Center Point Large Print
600 Brooks Road / PO Box 1
Thorndike ME 04986-0001 USA

(207) 568-3717

US & Canada:
1 800 929-9108
www.centerpointlargeprint.com

ACKNOWLEDGMENTS

Surround yourselves with good people. Every day John Morris Sr. and John Morris Jr. (Toot), along with Robert Steppe, come to work on the farm. They are a joy. Dana Flaherty, professional whipper-in, also manages the farm, and she frees me from many of the small burdens so I can concentrate on the larger. The hunt club members (we don't kill foxes so don't get your knickers in a knot) are the best people I know, and they carry me along.

But in many ways the deepest acknowlegments must go to my cats, dogs, horses, and hounds, for I connect often more intensely with these friends than I do with most humans. Perhaps I know their language better, who is to say? If there aren't cats, dogs, horses, hounds, and, of course, foxes, in heaven, I'm not going. Then again, I might not be going anyway. Curious, isn't it, that even in the afterlife humans have created an uptown and a downtown?

I couldn't live without my four-footed friends, and I couldn't write, either.

CAST OF CHARACTERS

Mary Minor "Harry" Haristeen — Formerly the postmistress of Crozet, she now is trying to make a go of it with farming. She turned forty in August and doesn't seem to mind.

Pharamond "Fair" Haristeen, D.V.M. — Harry's husband is an equine vet, and he tries to keep his wife out of trouble, with limited success.

Susan Tucker — Harry's best friend since cradle days, who often marvels at how Harry's mind works, when it works. The two of them know each other so well that, if they wished, one could finish the other's sentences.

Mrs. Miranda Hogendobber — Miranda observes a great deal but keeps most of it to herself. She's in her early seventies, devoutly Christian, and mothers Harry, who lost her own mother when she was in her twenties.

Marilyn "Big Mim" Sanburne — The Queen of Crozet sees all and knows all, or would like to, at any rate. She despotically improves everyone's lot but is good-hearted underneath it all.

Aunt Tally Urquhart — This wild woman, in her nineties, must be a devotee of the god Pan, for she's in her glory when pandemonium reigns. She's Big Mim's aunt and delights in shocking her prim niece.

Deputy Cynthia Cooper — Harry's neighbor, she, like Fair, tries to keep Harry out of trouble when she can. She's smart and likes law enforcement.

Sheriff Rick Shaw — He's the dedicated public servant, insightful but by the book. He wearies of the politics of his position, but he never wearies of bringing criminals to justice. He likes Harry, but she gets in the way.

Olivia "BoomBoom" Craycroft — She was widowed in her early thirties and, being quite beautiful, always trailed troops of men behind her. One of them was Fair Haristeen, who had an affair with her when he was separated from Harry. He and Harry have since divorced and remarried. BoomBoom can be forceful when necessary.

Alicia Palmer — A great movie star, now in her fifties, she's thrilled to be back on the farm in Crozet. She's also thrilled that she's found BoomBoom, for they truly connect.

THE REALLY IMPORTANT CHARACTERS

Mrs. Murphy — She's a pretty tiger cat with brains, speed, and a reasonably tolerant temperament. She knows she can't really keep Harry, her human, out of trouble, but she can sometimes get her out once she's in a mess.

Tee Tucker — This corgi, also devoted to Harry, has great courage and manages to live with two cats. That says a lot.

Pewter — The gray cannonball, as she does not like to be known, affects disdain for humans. However, she loves Harry and Fair. If it's possible to avoid a long way or trouble, she's the first to choose that path.

Simon — Living in the barn with all the horses pleases this possum. He also likes Harry, as much as he can like humans. She gives him treats.

Flatface — Sharing the loft with Simon, this great horned owl looks down on earthbound creatures, figuratively and literally. However, in a pinch, Flatface can be counted on.

Matilda — She's a big blacksnake and the third roommate in the barn loft. Her sense of humor borders on the black, too.

Owen — Tee Tucker's brother belongs to Susan Tucker, who bred the litter. He doesn't know how his sister can tolerate the cats. When in feline company, he behaves, but he thinks the cats are snobs.

Since Mrs. Murphy, Tucker, and Pewter live on a farm, various creatures cross their path, from bears to foxes to one nasty blue jay. They love all the horses, which can't be said for some of the other creatures, but then, the horses are domesticated. Pewter declares she is not domesticated but merely resting in a house with regular meals.

1

St. Luke's, a beautiful stone church on the outskirts of Crozet, Virginia, appeared even more stunning than usual given the fresh snow on the rooftops, the windowsills of the parish office, and the pastor's living quarters across the now-white quad. Plumes of smoke rose from the great hall, which formed one side of the quad, and smoke spiraled from the parish office. The church was built in 1803, and it was clear that those early Lutherans needed many fireplaces. Over the centuries the buildings had been wired, vented, and plumbed. The modern conveniences served to enhance comfort. The structures had to last for centuries and no doubt would endure more improvements over ensuing centuries.

As Harry Haristeen walked across the large quad to the great hall, her two cats and corgi behind her, she wondered if people today could build as securely as our forefathers did. Seemed like things were built to fall apart. Grateful that she lived in an old farmhouse built about the same time as the church, she paused on her way to the work party long enough to make a snowball and throw it up in the air.

Tucker, the corgi, jumped up to catch it. As she did, the snowball chilled her teeth, so she dropped it.

"*Dumb!*" Pewter, the portly gray cat, laughed.

"*I knew it would do that, but if she throws a ball, I have to catch it. That's my job,*" Tucker defended herself.

Harry decided to sprint the last two hundred yards to warm up.

The tiger cat, Mrs. Murphy, shot past her. The shoveled walkway was covered with inches of fresh snow but easily negotiable.

Pewter, hating to be outdone, couldn't get around Harry so she leapt onto the snow, where she promptly sank.

Tucker, trotting on the path, called out, "*Dumb.*"

A snow triangle like a coolie hat on her head did not cool down Pewter's temper. She shook off the snow hat, plowed onto the path. Running right up to Tucker's butt, she reached out and gave the dog a terrific swat.

Tucker growled, stooped to whirl around.

Harry commanded over her shoulder, "That's enough, you two."

"You're lucky she saved your fat rear end." Pewter flattened her ears to look extra mean.

"Ooh la." The dog now ignored the cat, which was far more upsetting than a knock-down/drag-out to Pewter, who felt the world revolved around her.

Upon entering the great hall, Harry inhaled the fragrance of oak burning in the two fireplaces, one at either end. The aroma of a well-tended fire added to winter's allure. Harry loved all the seasons. Winter's purity appealed to her. She loved being able to see the spine of the land, loved popping into a friend's house for a hot chocolate or serving the same. Born and raised here, she was buoyed up by close friendships. People might feel alienated in big cities, but she couldn't imagine that emotion. Tied to the land, the people and animals that inhabited it, Harry knew she was a lucky soul.

"Look at those hardworking women," she called out as she removed her coat, hat, gloves, and scarf.

Alicia Palmer and BoomBoom Craycroft, both great beauties, moved a long table near the eastern fireplace. The large room cost so much to heat that the thermostat stayed at fifty-two. The fireplaces helped considerably.

Sitting near one kept one's fingers from stiffening, and they'd need their fingers today.

Alicia, a former movie star, now in her fifties, was in charge of decorations for the Christmas party, which was little more than a week away. Each season St. Luke's hosted a large party that brought parishioners and neighbors together in a relaxed setting. Reverend Herb Jones, the pastor, constantly came up with ways to strengthen the community.

Susan Tucker, Harry's best friend from cradle days, and the breeder of Tucker, put grapevines on the table.

Racquel Deeds and Jean Keelo, two former sorority sisters from Miami University in Ohio, laid out gorgeous dried magnolia grand flora blossoms along with the large, shiny dark-green leaves.

BoomBoom brought bay leaves and gold-beaded strands.

Harry carried dried red roses along with strands of cranberries.

Once the women settled down at the table to make wreaths, the cats and dog volunteered to help.

Mrs. Murphy, on the table, played with the gold beads. *"Aren't these the same kind of beads that men throw to women at Mardi Gras if the women expose their glories?"*

"Sure won't be flashing anything in this weather." Tucker, on the floor, laughed.

Pewter batted around a lovely red rosebud. *"I will never understand why humans pitch a fit and fall in it if someone shows their breasts or if a man shows his equipment. I mean, everybody has them."*

"Genesis. Remember when the angel comes to the Garden of Eden after Adam eats the apple and Adam and Eve realize they are naked?" Mrs. Murphy read over Harry's shoulder, not that Harry knew the cat could fathom it.

"Ha. Adam was taking money under the table from the garment industry." Pewter swept her tail over the table, knocking rosebuds on the floor.

"If you don't behave, missy, you're going on the floor," Harry chided Pewter.

"If you give me treats, I'll be an angel."

"Liar, liar, your pants are on fire," Mrs. Murphy sassed.

That fast, Pewter charged the tiger cat, the gold beads entangled between them. The two boxed. Harry stood up, separating the cats to save the beads.

Off the table, the two chased each other around the room.

"Anyone bring Valium for cats?" asked BoomBoom.

"Remind me next time to stock up," Harry replied.

Racquel and Jean had married best friends, and both couples had moved to Crozet when Bryson Deeds took a slot in the cardiology department at the University of Virginia hospital. He'd gone on to become one of the leading cardiologists in the country. Bill Keelo, his best friend, specialized in tax law. He, too, flourished. Both men earned very good money, and their wives reflected being well-tended. Of the two, Racquel was obsessed with her looks and appearing young.

While both wives were very attractive, any woman paled next to Alicia or BoomBoom. The funny thing was, neither of these great beauties fussed over themselves all that much, which only made them more alluring.

Harry, good-looking but not drop-dead gorgeous, lived in jeans. Since she farmed, this was as it should be, but every now and then Alicia, BoomBoom, and Susan would gang up on her and drag her to stores to find dresses. It took three of them to make her do it.

Although Racquel and Jean had not grown up with everyone, they had lived in Crozet for twenty years, fitting right in.

"You know, this really is lovely." Susan

held up a wreath of magnolia leaves, white magnolia blossoms, red rosebuds, and gold beads wrapped diagonally around the wreath.

"This looks pretty good, too. A little more plain, perhaps." Harry held up the bay leaf wreath with cranberries wrapped around it, set off with large pale-green bows and speckled with tiny gold stars.

"The odor. That's what makes the bay leaf wreaths so special." Jean adored the fragrance.

"What are we going to do with the grapevines?" Susan was twisting some, now pliable from being soaked in water, into lovely wreaths.

"Well, I thought we could put one big bow on the bottom and tie in the wooden carved figures from that plastic carton." Alicia pointed to the carton.

Susan asked, "Want me to do that now?"

Alicia answered, "No, let's make the wreaths for the outside doors. By that time we should be able to handle the two huge wreaths for in here."

"How huge?" Harry wondered.

"Three feet in diameter," Alicia replied.

"That is huge." Harry was surprised.

"It will take two of us to make each one, then hang them over each fireplace, but they will look spectacular." Alicia felt confident about that.

One of the outside doors opened. Rushing in were the three Lutheran cats, Cazenovia, Elocution, and Lucy Fur, followed by Herb Jones, wearing no coat.

"Rev, you'll catch your death." Harry called him Rev.

"Oh, I just ran over from the office." He glanced at the few finished wreaths and the pile of materials on the table as the cats, now five in number, roared through the great hall. "These are so pretty."

"Thought about adding walnuts, but I don't think they'd last long." BoomBoom pointed to the grapevine wreaths. "Alicia's come up with other ideas. She's the boss."

"I'm grateful to you girls for doing this." Herb smiled at them. "Do you all need anything? Food? Drink?"

"Brought it," Jean replied. "Dip into either of those coolers. You'll be happy."

Rarely able to resist food, Herb flipped up both lids. "Are those your famous turkey and cranberry sandwiches?"

"The same," Jean replied.

Herb picked out one, as well as a Coca-Cola. "I'm going to eat and run. Actually, I'll eat in the office. Oh, Racquel, how's Aunt Phillipa doing?"

"Thank God for the Brothers of Love Hospice. Her mind remains clear, but I doubt she'll make it to spring. Emphysema takes you down." Racquel looked up at him.

Jean added, "The brothers have been wonderful. Apart from the work they do with the dying, it's inspirational to learn each monk's history. Everyone is there to atone for some wrongdoing."

Racquel said, "Atoning twice. Some have been in jail."

"Do you really think a leopard can change his spots?" Harry, ever the questioner, said.

Herb replied in a deep voice, "Some can and some can't. I doubt it's easy, and as I recall most of them were first corrupted by greed or lust."

"Women and song pushed them on the path," Susan good-naturedly suggested.

Herb turned to leave, noticing the cats carrying on like sin. "Jean, a turkey sandwich, if you have an extra, might settle these hellions down."

"Brought plenty. Would you like another?"

"No, this is fine." He left to dash back across the quad.

Alicia rose to throw more logs onto the fire, the fireplace being quite large to accommodate the big room. "Harry, I'd like to think people can change."

"I would, too, but it seems to me that some corruptions are more easily overcome than others." Harry selected a deep-red rosebud.

"Sex. That's harder to fix than greed. Or should I say lust?" Racquel said.

"Really? I think money trumps everything in our culture," Susan replied.

"I don't think so." Racquel offered her argument in the best sense of the word. "Lust is irrational. The desire for money is rational."

"But aren't the seven deadly sins all irrational? I mean, when it gets to that level of an obsession." BoomBoom, like most people among friends, didn't mind taking a bit of grammatical license.

Important as good grammar can be, it can also be stultifying in free-flowing conversation.

"Okay. How do you know when it's reached the level of obsession?" Harry liked to talk about ideas, not people.

"Maybe it's different for each person," Jean offered.

BoomBoom, whose husband died young, had entered into a string of affairs with men, one of whom was Fair Haristeen, D.V.M., Harry's husband. They were separated at the time, and Harry subsequently divorced him. He worked on himself, kept after her for years once he recognized his error, and finally won her back. Nothing happens in a vacuum. Harry had to realize that she contributed to his wandering by focusing on whatever tasks presented themselves to her. She could have focused on him a little more. She was learning.

"Wouldn't a sign be if you knew you should slow down but you speeded up?" The corgi added canine conversation to this topic.

Just then, led by Mrs. Murphy, the cats leapt onto the table, running from end to end. Grapevines hit the floor; rosebuds skidded off the table. BoomBoom quickly secured the magnolia blossoms, as they were more fragile. Beads clattered.

"I'm sorry. I should never have brought these monsters," Harry apologized.

"Oh, the Rev's cats would have done the honors." BoomBoom, an animal lover, laughed.

What was a little cleanup compared to watching animals love life?

"We would not. We're Christian cats," Lucy Fur protested, prudently jumping off the table.

"Ha." Pewter jumped off, too. *"Lucy Fur, you're the most Christian at dinnertime."*

"You should talk, lard-ass." Cazenovia, the long-haired calico, now chased Pewter.

"May I?" Harry got up and opened the cooler.

"Under the circumstances, I think it imperative." Jean smiled.

Once the torn-up sandwich was on the floor, paper towels underneath, the cats settled down. Tucker received half a sandwich, too. Water was put out for them.

The great hall boasted a kitchen good enough for a fancy restaurant; it had running water, a Sub-Zero refrigerator, a big Viking stove, and other items to delight a chef.

Back at the table, Harry plopped down.

"Those sandwiches smell good." Susan's remark encouraged the ladies to take a food break.

"You mentioned that Aunt Phillipa's mind is clear. How is she taking this?" Alicia asked Racquel.

"With fortitude. She's eighty-six. She's ready to go. Fighting to breathe robs any delight one might harbor. But she amazes me. So do the brothers. I didn't think I'd much like them hovering about, but they've been good. Well, Christopher Hewitt isn't too good. Brother Morris," she mentioned the prior, "says he has to do some hospice work. Mostly Christopher runs the Christmas tree farm. He knows how to make money. Bryson is there more than I am, so Aunt Phillipa receives lots of attention. He has two elderly patients there, as well."

BoomBoom, who'd gone to high school with Christopher, as did Harry, Fair, and Susan, said, "I haven't seen Christopher since he joined the brotherhood. Not that we were bosom buddies before."

"Heard he became a brother after he got out of jail in Arizona. Money led him down the garden path. I am going over to the Christmas tree farm later, and maybe he'll be there." Harry was looking forward to picking out a tree.

Susan spoke to Alicia, Racquel, and Jean, who did not go to Crozet High School. "Christopher was a year behind Harry and me. He was handsome. And he was always elected treasurer of whatever group he was in."

"Good training." BoomBoom laughed.

"That comes back to my question," said Harry. "Can a leopard change his spots? I don't know all of the details, but Christopher was a stockbroker, became involved in insider trading, losing millions of clients' money. I just wonder."

"Well, I changed my spots." BoomBoom laughed again, at herself this time.

"Oh, you were never that bad." Susan liked her school chum, although she sided with

Harry during the affair, which was natural.

"Bad enough." Harry laughed, too. "But isn't it funny how things turn out? All three of us have grown closer."

BoomBoom became serious. "The truth is I didn't know what love was until I met Alicia. I was running on empty and running from man to man."

"You sweet thing," Alicia said.

Racquel, not one to hold back, asked, "Think you were always gay?"

"No. Not for a second. I don't even know if I am now, but I love Alicia. If that makes me gay, I'm happy to claim it. But, Racquel, I never once thought about another woman that way." She turned to Jean. "Which reminds me, I'm surprised Bill allows you to work with Alicia and me."

Jean rolled her eyes. "He's gotten worse. He's not as bad about two women as two men, but he's really become a bigot. The other thing that sets him off is illegal immigration." She looked around at the others. "The man I married was purposeful but fun. I don't know — he entered his forties and now he's such a crab. I hasten to add that he's good to me. But he really loathes anything and everything about gay men. I just don't know what to do about it, because there are gay men in our social groups. He avoids them."

"Not a thing you can do." Racquel shrugged, then tossed a rosebud at Harry. "The leopard and his spots. I worry about Bryson. He says he's changed, but I don't know. These last few months I kind of get the feeling he's slipping back. I've checked the new nurses. None is his type."

"Racquel, there hasn't been a whiff of gossip, and you know that the hospital is a hotbed of it. If he were sleeping with a nurse, we'd know." Jean wanted Racquel to be happy.

"I'd have heard." Susan did hear a lot, plus her husband — a lawyer — served as a representative in the Virginia legislature and was on the hospital board.

"I don't know." Racquel appeared glum for a minute. "I swear to you, if he is fooling around and I catch him, that is one man who will be singing soprano in the choir."

All the women laughed at this, each knowing, however fleetingly, that thought of revenge.

Pewter and the others had been listening. *"I'm not changing my spots."*

"You don't have any spots." Tucker laughed at her.

"You know what I mean." Pewter stared crossly at the dog.

"That you think you're perfect," Tucker said.

"I'm glad you recognize that." Pewter beamed as the other cats laughed.

2

A string of red and green lightbulbs, supported by four poles, formed a square shining down on rows of freshly cut Christmas trees. The Brothers of Love kept a tight grasp on the wallet. No need to squander funds on fancy lights or even a crèche. The Christmas tree farm provided the brothers with half their annual income.

The square rows of Scotch pines undulated, roots balled and in large pots. Other trees, still planted, would be dug up after the shopper selected one. A forklift put the pots of freshly dug trees into truck beds. Sliding a potted tree into a station wagon proved more difficult, since the root balls were quite heavy, but after ten years the brothers had it down to a science.

People flocked to the tree farm because the trees were symmetrical and the prices fair. One also left the farm feeling smugly virtuous, since the money did fund their hospice.

Back in the early 1980s, when even some medical personnel wouldn't touch AIDS patients because the transmission of the disease was not fully understood, the brothers formed to nurse the sick and comfort the dying. Their commitment to all patients regardless of disease won them respect and support. The order wore monks' habits, a black rope tying them tight around the middle. This outward display of their vows, in these secular times, pushed some people away from them. Others rushed toward them, eager to bare sins. By starting the hospice, perhaps the brothers wished to spare themselves such repetitive boredom. What each brother learned over time was that there are no original sins.

Harry Haristeen walked through the trees outside the square. Sticking close to her were Mrs. Murphy and Pewter, both nimbly stepping over garlands and wreaths that had been laid to the side, SOLD tags attached to them.

Popping out from an aisle of trees off the small main square was Alex Corbett, head of Corbett Realty.

"Harry, find a tree?"

"Not yet. You?"

"A big one. Need an impressive specimen for the annual company party."

"Same night as St. Luke's. Bad timing." She smiled.

"Oh, Harry, people party all day and night. Half of the St. Luke's people will come over to Keswick Club. I'm counting on you and Fair to add to the celebration."

"Alex, we'd love to, but I've got to help clean up."

His sandy mustache twitched upward. "Well, I'll see you at Spring Fling, then." He waved good-bye as he walked to his new Range Rover and drove off.

She said to her animals, "Real estate has been tanking for two years and yet that man rolls in the dough. Wish I had his brains for money."

"You have a good brain," Tucker complimented her.

As it was two in the afternoon on December 15, she had the farm all to herself once Alex left. The high volume of shoppers would fill the place after work. The other women at the work party had their trees up already, but Harry, like her mother, waited until ten days before Christmas.

Tucker patiently examined each tree. Had to smell right.

"Pine" — Pewter sniffed — *"all smells the same."*

"Does not," the sturdy dog replied.

"I don't want to hear about your superior nose. My nose is every bit as good as yours."

Although Tucker knew she was being goaded, an activity at which Pewter excelled, she couldn't help herself. She rose to the bait. *"My nose is superior. Why, I can track a cow on a three-day-old line."*

"Ooh la." Pewter tossed back her head. *"Even a bloodhound can't do that. Furthermore, what do you want with a stinky cow? The cud breath could gag a maggot."*

The fur on the back of her neck fluffed up as Tucker responded, *"You don't know anything about canine noses."*

"Well, I know all I need to know about canine butts, you tailless wonder." Pewter giggled.

Tucker whirled around, ready for a fight. The dog had endured five lunatic cats at St. Luke's. Her feline fun meter was pegged.

Mrs. Murphy stopped to face them as Harry walked on, and said with an authoritative voice, *"Can it."*

Rarely did Tucker oppose the tiger cat. They were good friends. Besides, Murphy could unleash those claws and tear her up.

Pewter, while not wishing to tangle with the tiger, didn't want to look as though she'd backed down. *"Who died and made you God?"*

Upset at her phrase, Tucker said, *"You*

shouldn't talk like that. We just came from St. Luke's. Besides, there are brothers around."

Mrs. Murphy couldn't help but laugh at Tucker's seriousness. *"Since when do humans understand our language? Even our own human doesn't get it."*

"Right." Pewter seized on what she took to be a tiny bit of support from Mrs. Murphy. *"Furthermore, most of the brothers are mental. They're making up for something. You know, atoning for sins. Why would anyone want to sit with the dying? It's not normal."*

"Pewter, you're hateful." Mrs. Murphy turned to follow Harry, who was attractive even in a dirty, smeared Carhartt work jacket.

"I tell the truth. Why is that being hateful?" Pewter yelled to the two animals leaving her. *"They're a bunch of whack jobs."*

As Tucker padded along next to Mrs. Murphy, she said, *"Her nose gets out of joint because she doesn't like the cold. Does she stay in the truck? No. She lives in fear that she'll miss something and then all she does is bitch and moan."*

A gray cannonball shot past them. Pewter turned to face them after skidding to a stop, sending pine needles flying. *"You're talking about me!"*

"Egotist," Tucker fired back.

"As it happens, we were. We were discussing how you hate the cold but you won't stay in the truck," said Mrs. Murphy.

"Ha. You were saying ugly things about me. Un-Christian things."

"Pewter." Both Mrs. Murphy and Tucker said the same thing at the same time while laughing at the cross kitty.

Harry, hearing the chatter, called to her friends, "Come on, you all, keep up."

"It's her fault." Tucker petulantly pointed the paw, so to speak, at Pewter.

Pewter hopped sideways, stiff-legged, toward the dog. Then she swatted the corgi.

"That's enough," Harry commented. "Look at this one."

"Very nice." Tucker admired the twelve-foot tree, which would look good in the old farmhouse with its high ceilings.

"Can't wait to climb it," Pewter said.

"Have to wait until it's decorated. Maximum damage," Mrs. Murphy gleefully ordered.

"Where is everybody?" Harry wondered out loud. "Ought to be a brother around here somewhere."

"Probably in prayer and penance." Pewter sarcastically giggled.

Harry misinterpreted Pewter's remarks, thinking the cat wanted to be picked up. She bent over, hoisting the large cat.

Given that a free ride beat walking, Pewter didn't fuss.

Tucker raced down the row of trees, reached the end, and raced back in another tree lane. She continued running up and back while the others returned to the square.

Just as Harry and the cats reached the lighted open square, she noticed an SUV pulling away. She walked to the small trailer and knocked on the door.

"Just a minute," a male voice called from inside.

The flimsy door opened. Out stepped a man in his late thirties, wearing the winter habit, a heavy brown wool robe. His red beard and mustache were offset by bright blue eyes.

Harry paused, finally recognized who it was behind the beard, then said, "Christopher Hewitt, we were just talking about you."

He smiled. "It's been years since I've seen you, Harry. And who's 'we'?"

She hugged him, then let go. "The decorating committee at St. Luke's. You remember Susan Tucker and BoomBoom Craycroft. They were there. I don't think you know the other ladies."

"You know what Mae West said? The only thing worse than being talked about is not being talked about. So what did they say?"

"That you'd joined the brotherhood after being in the slammer."

"Heard I made the papers back home." He ruefully smiled. "Took my vows a year ago plus a few days. I needed to completely change my life. I'd made a terrible mistake. Anyway, I give myself to service. Perhaps, in time, the good I do will outweigh the bad."

"It will." She reassured him. "We all make mistakes."

"Mine cost other people millions."

"Yes, well" — she laughed — "that is a major mistake."

"I don't do things halfway." He pulled his hands back into the heavy sleeve. "Would you like to come into the trailer? Warm."

"Thanks. I want to buy a tree. Can you tag it for me?"

"Sure."

They walked to the perfectly shaped tree that Harry had marked. Chris pulled a red cardboard tag from a pocket in his robe. "There you go."

"Aren't your hands cold?"

"Yes. I try to keep to the tradition — no gloves, no shoes — but I surely wear gloves and shoes when it's cold."

"No shoes?"

"Sandals. We can wear sandals, but I cheat and wear Thinsulate-lined boots when it's this cold. Really is cold, too. I think we'll have a white Christmas."

He stepped back to admire the tree. "Remember old Mr. Truslow, who used to show *White Christmas* every year in assembly? I thought it was the most boring movie I'd ever seen, but at least we were out of the classroom."

"Really? I liked it." She paused. "I think he showed it to us because he was in the war. The idea of a reunion and all that."

"Maybe. Want me to put the tree in your truck?"

"No, thanks, because Fair can't get here until about nine. I want to make sure he likes the tree. Half of making a marriage work is letting your spouse in on every decision."

"Another mistake I made. My wife bailed when the scandal broke about insider trading. I wished she'd loved me enough to stick it out, but I can't say that I blame her." He sighed.

"I'm sorry."

"Me, too. I was a fool. How much is enough? Made millions, Harry, millions, and I wanted more. I was a fool. Like I said, I hope the good I do now will make up for what I did then."

"Will." She walked back to her old truck.

"These old Fords go and go. When did you get it?" He walked around it, noticing the good condition of the F-series truck.

"When I graduated from Smith, in 1990."

His gaze ran over the '78 Ford again. "I miss my Porsche." He shrugged. "Funny how you can love an inanimate object."

"Makes sense to me." She opened the truck door.

The cats hopped in, but she had to pick up Tucker.

"Good to see you, Harry. I'll be here until ten. If you and Fair run late, call." He waved as she drove off.

Heading toward the farm, she thought that the leopard could change his spots if he truly was motivated.

At least that's what she figured.

"Where are we going?" Pewter wanted a nap.

"We're here," Mrs. Murphy said as Harry drove down the alleyway behind the old post office, where she used to work.

Once parked in Miranda Hogendobber's driveway off the alleyway, she paused to notice that even in the snow, Miranda's gardens, symmetrically laid out, still pleased the eye.

"Knock knock." She opened the back door.

"Come on in. I'm in the living room," Miranda, Harry's surrogate mother and former workmate at the post office, called out.

The animals dashed in to be rapturously greeted, followed by Harry, who received a big hug and kiss.

"Wow." Harry admired Miranda's tree.

"Thought I'd do something different this year."

"It's gorgeous."

A Douglas fir, reaching the ceiling, bore evidence of Miranda's highly developed aesthetic sensibility. Plaid bows, shot through with some gold thread, were tied in place of balls. A lush gold garland wrapped around the tree. On the top, a single thin gold star finished the picture.

"You really like it? I haven't been too severe?"

"I love it."

"Sit down. Tea?"

"I'm on the run. Just wanted to stop by. We made the wreaths today. Are you nervous?"

"A little." She chuckled. "A lot."

"You'll be fab."

Miranda, a stalwart at the Church of the Holy Light, had agreed to sing at St. Luke's Christmas party on the winter solstice. Her partner would be none other than Brother Morris, formerly a major tenor in the opera world.

"We've practiced. Brother Morris puts me at ease, but, Harry, that voice." She threw her hands heavenward. "A gift from God."

"So is yours."

"Now, now. Flatterer."

"Miranda, people wouldn't have asked you to sing with Brother Morris if you didn't have the stuff."

"Oh, Herbie asked me."

"He's a good judge."

She changed the subject. "Visited Phillipa Henry. Sinking fast."

Racquel's aunt had moved to the area when Racquel and Bryson did. Childless, the woman doted on her niece and Racquel's two sons.

"Racquel said as much."

"You know, I've never been to the Brothers of Love Hospice before. They do God's work."

"I believe they do."

Harry told her about seeing Christopher Hewitt. They caught up on odds and ends, the glue of life in the country and small towns.

"Another thing." Miranda returned to Aunt Phillipa. "Bryson was there. He stops by and visits Phillipa. Brother Luther was there, too, and says that Bryson makes a point of visiting each of the people in their care. I was impressed with how tender he was. I mean, since he's . . . uh" — even though she was with Harry, she still paused, since a Southern lady is not to speak ill of anyone — "full of himself."

"He is that." Harry laughed. "But I guess to be really successful at anything, you need a big ego."

"I conclude he's very successful." They both laughed, then Miranda added, "He seemed distant and tense. Not with the patients but in general."

"Racquel's suspicious."

"I hope that's unfounded." Miranda shook her head. "Truly."

"Me, too. How do people find the time for affairs? One man is all I can do."

"Me, too."

"Tell me what you think. We got into a discussion at St. Luke's. Started about the Brothers of Love, how each man is trying to change, to make up for past sins. Do you think the leopard can change his spots?"

"Of course. One asks for Christ's help, but, of course, Jesus represents change. Rebirth."

"Never thought of it that way."

"Honey, you're a good woman, but you don't have a religious turn of mind."

"I don't need it. You do it for me."

They laughed again, then Harry kissed her on the cheek and went on her way.

3

The air was cold. The sun had long set, so the cold intensified. The tiny square of red and green lights appeared more festive than it had at two in the afternoon. Eleven people, three of them children, studied the cut Christmas trees with varying degrees of seriousness.

Pewter elected to remain in the truck, where she snuggled into an ancient cashmere throw. Mrs. Murphy and Tucker tagged along, little puffs of frosty air streaming from their nostrils.

A child's shrill voice asserted, "Daddy, get this one."

Harry looked to see the source.

A child, perhaps ten, wanted a beautifully shaped Scotch pine. From the look of his clothing and the expression on his father's face, the tree must have been beyond the budget.

The economy was tanking and the high gas

prices pinched pocketbooks. Harry felt a pang that the child had selected a lovely tree that his father couldn't afford. She thought for a moment to buy the tree for him. On second thought, no. The kid had to learn about money. Better sooner than later.

Rolling his big tree on a dolly, Alex Corbett stopped for a breather near father and son. Reaching into his pocket, he pulled out a $100 bill, folded it in his palm, then pressed it into the father's hand.

Before the man could respond, Alex lifted the dolly and rolled away.

Fair called out to him, "Hold up, Alex. I'll help you load."

The two men maneuvered the tree to the Range Rover, then with effort hoisted it into the back, tying down the rear door since the tree stuck out.

"Thanks, Fair. Brother Sheldon is on overload." He shook Fair's hand.

"I'll take the dolly back," Fair offered.

"Hey, want to bet on the Sugar Bowl?" Alex beamed.

Fair amiably refused. "No. I don't know enough about either team."

Fair inhaled the scent of pine and cut wood as he left the dolly by the trailer. He rejoined his wife. They'd known each other since childhood, and he couldn't imagine life without her.

"Honey, who's playing in the Sugar Bowl?"

"I don't know," she replied.

Brother Sheldon, harried, tried to keep up with the customers.

Harry waited for an opportune moment to speak to him. "Is Brother Christopher here?"

"He's supposed to be, but I can't find him." Exasperation oozed from every pore.

Like Christopher, Brother Sheldon wore the heavy winter brown robe. He had socks on with his sandals. In his fifties, Brother Sheldon had converted from Reform Judaism to Christianity. The other brothers occasionally teased him about Jews for Jesus, which he bore with good grace.

"I know you're busy," Harry said. "I picked out our tree this afternoon. I want Fair to look at it. If he likes it, we can load it up and pay for it."

"Fine."

"It's one of the balled ones."

His eyebrows came together. "I'll need the front-end loader. Might take some time."

"Tell you what. Don't worry about it. It's in the back. We'll check it out. If it stays busy, I'll come back tomorrow."

Relief flooded over his pleasant, roundish features. "I hate for you to do that, but I sure appreciate it."

"Brother, Crozet's not but so big. Easy to come back."

Tucker walked back with Harry at her heels. Fair recognized a client behind one of the trees that were leaning against wooden railings. They chatted about the man's big crossbred mare.

Harry knew the fellow, too — Olsen Godfrey. After the pleasantries were exchanged, she took Fair back to see the tree.

Mrs. Murphy, who'd stayed with Fair, fell in with Tucker.

The farther away they walked from the lighted square, the darker it became. On her truck key chain, Harry had a tiny LED light. They reached the tree and she shone the light on it.

"What do you think?"

"It's a beautiful tree. A real evergreen pyramid." Fair put his arm around his wife's waist and said, "You have a good eye."

Tucker lifted her nose. *"Delicious."*

Mrs. Murphy inhaled deeply. *"Fresh."*

The two scooted off.

"Hey!" Harry called to them.

"We'll be right back," Tucker called over her shoulder.

"This tree is so perfect — the apotheosis of Christmas trees." Harry admired it.

"Even if for some reason I didn't like it, bet you someone else would." Fair lifted one side of the ball. "Heavy, but I think I can get it to the truck."

"Honey, don't. You're strong as a bull, but maybe Brother Sheldon would let you borrow the forklift."

"Good idea."

They hadn't taken two steps toward the square when Tucker ran past them. She carried her head to the side, something in her mouth.

Mrs. Murphy, in hot pursuit, called out, *"I told you to leave it. You're going to get us in a lot of trouble."*

Tucker refused to answer lest she drop her prize.

Harry yelled, "Tucker, what have you got?"

"She stole it." Mrs. Murphy blew past Tucker and turned to face the dog, but Tucker, with corgi agility, leapt to the side, avoiding the swift paw.

Fair sprinted toward the powerful, low-built dog. "Tucker, drop it."

Hearing that bass voice commanding her, Tucker did release her treasure. Standing over it, she kept a glaring eye on Mrs. Murphy.

"I don't want the damned thing," Mrs. Murphy, eyes large, hissed.

Harry shone the LED light on the coveted object. "Black rope. It's what the monks use to tie their robes."

Fair stood up, all six feet five inches of him. "I'll give this to Brother Sheldon. Hate to think of a monk in undress." He laughed. Then he picked it up. "Sticky."

"Tucker, where'd you find this?" Harry asked.

Tucker led her two humans to the site.

"You just can't leave well enough alone."

"The blood smells so delicious."

Trotting through the long rows of planted trees, Tucker took them to the very back. Leaning against a huge, perfectly pyramidal tree was Christopher Hewitt. Eyes wide open, mouth agape, he appeared to be calling out.

Harry, using her little light, faltered a moment as she took in the scene.

Fair stopped, too. Then the vet in him took over. He checked for a pulse. He shook his head.

"The body is cooling. It's so cold out, though, I can't really estimate how long he's been dead. Shine that light here."

When the light hit Christopher's face, Harry moved it downward. She grimaced.

His throat had been so neatly sliced one barely noticed it. The dark brown of the robe matched the blood stains.

Fair flipped open his cell and called their neighbor, Deputy Cynthia Cooper, who was on duty tonight.

"Smells wonderful." Tucker lifted her nose to inhale the aroma of fresh blood.

"Poor guy. Poor guy," Harry repeated to herself.

"At least it was quick. Who would do such a thing?" Fair had been two years ahead of Christopher Hewitt in high school and hadn't known him well. "Shouldn't we tell Brother Sheldon?"

"Listen, for all we know, Brother Sheldon killed him. When we hear the sirens, we can walk out. No telling what he'll do if he is the murderer."

What he did was pass out.

Cooper arrived not ten minutes after Fair had worried that Brother Sheldon was the culprit. Those ten minutes seemed so long to Harry and Fair, standing still in the biting cold.

Cooper, having first checked out the scene, brought back Brother Sheldon. He keeled over without even bending at the knee.

She knelt down to lift him at the shoulders.

"Coop, let me," Fair said.

"Thanks. Get behind him to lift him, Fair. Sometimes they puke all over you."

Brother Sheldon didn't throw up; he simply passed out again.

"The hell with it." Coop gave her full attention to the scene.

"Whoever did this worked fast and knew what they were doing," Fair commented.

"How so?" Harry asked.

"It takes some power to cut through a throat. This is neat."

Cooper, plastic gloves on, carefully checked the body. "Doesn't appear there's trauma elsewhere." She pushed up his sleeves. No bruising appeared. The coroner would be the last word on this.

"He was turning his life around. He was so positive. I can't believe this." Harry was upset.

"Any ideas?" Cooper stood up.

"No," they replied in unison.

"It's bad enough to murder someone, but at Christmas." Harry felt both sorrow and outrage.

Brother Sheldon moaned.

"He'll come to when he's good and ready." Cooper shone her powerful flashlight on Sheldon's face. "Ought to be interesting when we find the killer."

"Why? I mean beyond finding out who did

it?" Harry wiggled her toes in her boots, because even with Thinsulate they were cold.

"Brothers of Love. Right? Can they forgive the killer?"

Fair smelled that odd metallic tang of blood. "Better find him first. Then we can worry about forgiveness. It's a crying shame, really."

They heard the sirens. In the still of the night, sound carried. The sheriff's squad car and the forensic team's car had just driven under the railroad overpass and were now heading north.

"How do you know the people you told to stay here won't leave?" Harry considered the shoppers standing in the lighted square.

"If they go, they'll be suspect, which I made abundantly clear. I also took the precaution of punching their license plates into my computer." Cooper kept a laptop in her squad car, as did the other officers.

"Smart." Fair nodded.

"Procedure. Get as much information as you can as fast as you can without being obvious. People like to complain about the department, but then, people like to complain, period. We're well trained."

Brother Sheldon, laid out like a log, nearly tripped Sheriff Rick Shaw, whose eyes immediately darted to the tree, then back to Brother Sheldon.

"Is he dead?" Rick asked about Brother Sheldon as three other law-enforcement people walked with him, one with a camera.

"No. Where's Buddy?" Cooper meant the regular crime-scene photographer, who was a freelancer.

Well prepared as the department was, the struggle for an adequate budget did create problems.

"Doak will do it," Rick said, then added, "Why would anyone take out a monk?"

Doak called out from behind his camera. "Shine more light here, will you?"

The other members of the sheriff's department focused their flashlights on the corpse.

Rick crossed his arms over his chest. "Doak, when you're finished with the pictures, go get statements from the people up front. It's cold, and they'll want to go home."

"Any of them find the body?" Doak answered.

"No," Cooper responded. "Harry and Fair found it. Fair said the other person here who left with a tree was Alex Corbett. I'll question him later."

"I found it." Tucker puffed out her chest.

"Actually, Tucker and Mrs. Murphy found the body. Tucker brought the rope that tied his robe," Harry corrected the deputy.

"I really am going to have to put that dog and cat on the payroll." Rick smiled down at the two animals, then sighed. "Gang, looks like we'll be working harder than usual this holiday."

"I don't mind pulling extra hours," Cooper volunteered.

Rick looked down at Brother Sheldon. "Guess we'd better get him up. We need a statement."

Fair again hoisted up the brother, who weighed two hundred fifty pounds, much of it fat. Life was good at the monastery.

"Oh-h-h." Brother Sheldon's eyelids fluttered, then popped open.

"Gonna puke?" Rick asked.

"No." Tears rolled down the portly man's cheeks.

"I know this is difficult, but I must ask you some questions."

Brother Sheldon nodded.

"Do you need a drink or anything?" Fair asked. He usually carried a cooler in his truck, as he never knew how long he'd be on a call.

"No." Brother Sheldon shook his head.

"When was the last time you saw Brother Christopher?" Rick asked with a reassuring voice.

"Breakfast. He wasn't here when I arrived

at six. At first I thought he was digging up trees, balling them or putting them in buckets. We like to have a few that can be planted ready to go."

"Did you hear equipment?"

"No. The place filled up with people, so I didn't look too hard for him." Brother Sheldon cried. "I can't believe this. I just can't believe it."

"Do you have any ideas who might have done this?" Rick asked.

"Sheriff, he was relatively new to our order. A year, perhaps a few months more. He was in pain for having caused pain. When he came to us and accepted Christ, truly accepted Christ in his heart, he began to heal. He was such a likable man."

"He was. I can vouch for that, what I knew of him," Fair commented.

"You knew him from the monastery?" Rick continued scribbling in his open notebook.

"High school. He was two years behind me, a year behind my wife."

"Has anyone shown up at the monastery to speak to Brother Christopher that you hadn't seen before?" Rick kept prodding Brother Sheldon.

"No. People don't usually go up the mountain. Especially in winter. Roads are treacherous. If someone visits us, it's usually down at the hospice. Keeping the monastery separate allows us contemplation."

"I see. Brother Sheldon, go home." Rick patted him on the back. "Someone from the department will be up tomorrow to" — he chose his words carefully — "enlist help from the brothers. We will find whoever did this. I promise you, we will."

Tears again filled Brother Sheldon's eyes. "Think how this will upset children. Christmas is such a happy time, and the media will . . . well, you know how they are. Children don't need to know such things." He emitted a long, sorrowful sigh. "They're not allowed their innocence anymore."

"I agree, Brother, I agree." Rick patted him on the back again while giving a slight nod to Doak, who had returned from getting customers' statements.

Doak knew his boss's messages well. He gently put his hand under Brother Sheldon's elbow. "Come on, Brother. I'll take you to your car."

"I have to close up the place first."

"I'll help you. And if you need someone to drive you home, just tell me. A shock like this can make you wobbly."

"It can. I never imagined such a thing." The floodgates opened, and Doak walked with the brother back toward the lighted square.

Fair watched the slumping figure as the two men walked away. "Taking it hard."

Rick looked up at the tall vet. "Any ideas?"

"Only the obvious."

"Which is?"

"The killer is safe and sound and very effectively camouflaged."

"What makes you say that?" Cooper trusted Fair as a levelheaded person.

"Either he's miles down the road or he's sitting at home in Crozet, pleased with himself. This is a very cool customer. He walked right in here, killed quickly and silently, and walked right out without attracting notice."

"You're right." Rick smiled at Fair. "You might make a cop, know that?"

"Couldn't do it. But I'm a vet and I'm trained to observe without emotion if possible. Took some effort in this circumstance."

"It's always a shock when you know the victim," Rick repeated his earlier feeling.

Once back in the truck, Harry realized that they hadn't brought the tree. She'd lost her taste for it.

Mrs. Murphy and Tucker excitedly told Pewter everything.

Seething with envy, the gray cat grumbled, *"You lie."*

4

Brother Morris, head of the Brothers of Love, was so filled with the milk of human kindness that he almost mooed. Would have been a big moo, too, since Brother Morris tipped the scales at 310 pounds. Now forty-eight, he attracted devotees due to his own story. Once a major tenor in opera, specializing in German roles, he had fallen from grace. Given his weight, it was a wonder he didn't create a pothole in New York's streets big enough for three taxis to disappear altogether.

Most stars prove difficult at one time or another. Directors of opera houses learn to deal with egos as oversize as the voices. Gender seems not to be a determining factor. Of course, there are good and bad in every bunch, and Brother Morris, known then as Morris Bartoly, gave little trouble. He never fussed over the size of his dressing room or the placement of it. He appreciated large food baskets, especially fruit, for he loved to eat, and a bracing brandy assisted the digestion. However, he never showed up drunk, was always on time, and was perfectly willing to work with other stars far less generous in temperament than himself.

In short, he was a dream star, which made his crash all the more scandalous. Brother Morris slept with both men and women. Not that that was anything new. He often slept with them simultaneously, although how either gender bore the bulk remains mysterious. Discreet in his selections, Morris often chose partners who were married and slavish fans of opera. Few, if any, suspected his desires for threesomes. What did him in was not the number of playmates. One husband accepting Brother Morris's attentions just so happened to take pictures on his cell phone of the star servicing his wife, or was it vice versa? The sight of this behemoth performing various acts of copulation, dressed as a ballerina from *Swan Lake,* in specially made costumes, proved too much. The pictures on the cell phone showcased a thrilling dexterity for one so large. But, alas, when the news broke and he appeared onstage, he wasn't booed off, he was laughed off.

Brother Morris disappeared from the scene. A downward spiral of prostitutes and recreational drugs scuttled him. His taste for costumes became even more outrageous. He found Jesus when he landed in the gutter, dressed as Cleopatra, eyes heavily made up. Eschewing all publicity, he began to perform good works instead of tantric sex. He finally came to the Brothers of Love years later, where his energy and undeniable extroverted appeal made him invaluable, especially at the bedside of the dying.

When the founder of the Brothers of Love, Brother Price, formerly Price Newbold, died, it was a foregone conclusion that Brother Morris would become head of the order. He did. No one regretted the decision. In addition to his kindness to the dying, he showed fine managerial skills.

At this exact moment, those skills were in use. Officer Doak, worried about Brother Sheldon's condition, had driven him up Afton Mountain. Sheriff Shaw had given him the go-ahead to inform Brother Morris of events. It was up to Brother Morris to determine how to break this to "the boys," as he teasingly called them.

Brother Morris never got the chance. Brother Sheldon crossed the threshold of the monastery with such a wailing and weeping that everyone in their cells rushed out.

A monk's living quarters is traditionally

called a "cell," and these, while spare, did have heat and running water. No luxuries abounded, though.

He blurted out everything in lurid detail. Brother Morris, whose cell was farthest down the hall, arrived just as Brother Sheldon reached the pinnacle of his tale: the discovery of the body.

Horrified, he noticed the sheriff's man heading toward him.

"Brother Morris, could we talk in private?"

Nodding and then flicking his forefinger at Brother George, the second in command, he ushered Officer Doak into his office, where the young man told him what they'd found, with less drama than Brother Sheldon.

In defense of Brother Sheldon, how often do you find a man, murdered, propped up against a Christmas tree? However, Brother Sheldon flourished when his emotions expanded, so he was now in his glory.

"My God, this can't be true." Brother Morris's heavily bearded face became pale.

"I'm afraid it is, sir — I mean, Brother."

Brother Morris waved his hand. "Call me what you like. Have you any suspects?"

"No. But the investigation is just beginning. The forensics team will return at dawn since it's so dark now. I'm sorry, but we have to keep the Christmas tree farm closed for at least one more day."

"Small matter." He folded his hands together, bowed his head, then looked up. "What can I do to help you? We all loved Brother Christopher. Please let us help."

"We'll be back tomorrow to ask questions. That's a help, a beginning." Doak was soothing.

"Of course. Of course." Brother Morris's voice shook slightly.

"We will be questioning everyone involved." Officer Doak leaned forward slightly. "I know you are suffering a terrible shock, but I have a few questions now."

"I understand."

"Did Brother Christopher have any enemies in the order?"

Shaking his head vigorously, Brother Morris responded, "No, no, he was loved by all." He smiled slightly. "We are the Brothers of Love, but as you know, Officer, people do have trouble getting along. Not Brother Christopher. He was an easy fellow, and the love of Christ shone through him."

"Did anyone from the Christmas tree farm ever complain? A customer perhaps?"

"Not that I know of, but I will ask the other brothers."

Officer Doak rose. "Someone from the department will return tomorrow. I am sorry for your troubles, sir. We will do everything in our power to apprehend the murderer."

"I know you will. Go with God, Officer." A tear ran down his apple cheek into the grizzled beard. Doak passed through the long hall.

Once the officer left, in the front hall the noise had grown louder. Emotions ranged from stunned catatonia to Brother Sheldon ripping his shirt and fainting again. Brother Morris watched as Brother George fanned him.

"Brother Ed, go to the infirmary and fetch the smelling salts." Brother Morris stood to his full height of six foot two inches and said, "Brothers, horrible as this is, remember that Brother Christopher has gone home. He is with Christ, and we celebrate his release from this mortal coil. Brother Luther, you're in charge of a service for him, Friday. Brother Howard, you're in charge of the reception. Now" — a long pause followed — "does anyone have any ideas, know anything that might contribute to our understanding this loss?"

Blank looks met his request.

A tiny brother, a handsome former jockey who had hit the skids, piped up, "Maybe he didn't spend all the money."

"Say what?" Brother Morris seemed confused.

"Insider trading," Brother Speed, the jockey, replied. "He lost a lot of money for people. Have you ever heard of anyone who did such a thing not squirreling away a large bundle for themselves?"

Shocked, Brother Morris said, "He would have given it back."

Brother Speed, who knew a thing or two about crooks and scumbags, calmly stood his ground. "Now, Brother, I want to agree with you, but my hunch is that this all gets back to his stock-market days. There has to be a pile of money somewhere."

"Then why stay in the order?" Brother Luther was puzzled.

"For a cover. Maybe." Brother Speed shrugged. "I'm not saying this is the case. You asked for ideas."

Brother Morris stroked his beard. "Brother Speed, I hope you're wrong, but under the circumstances not one of us can rule out the possibility. If each of you would go jot down observations and thoughts, perhaps some pattern will emerge. In the meantime, I charge each of you to pray for Brother Chris's soul and to remember the love."

Brother Sheldon came to with a wail. Brother Morris sighed deeply, wishing Brother Sheldon was less histrionic. He'd lived through enough of that at the opera.

5

Dr. Emmanuel Gibson searched his memory for a similar case. Nothing came to mind. The seventy-five-year-old was a repository of pathology's secrets; younger doctors frequently consulted him. He was in good shape, with sharp skills, as he was usually called in when the regular coroner was unavailable.

Dr. Gibson examined the wound.

"There don't seem to be signs of struggle," Rick said.

"I need to send tissue samples off; haven't removed the organs yet." Dr. Gibson looked up from the corpse. "It's possible he was drugged — no struggle then."

Cooper nodded. "Like the date-rape drug."

Dr. Gibson examined the underside of the forearms to see if Christopher had warded off blows. "No marks. The severed jugular might have obscured fingerprints. If he was choked, his eyes would be bloodshot, and you'll notice they aren't."

Rick looked at the glassy, staring eyes. He couldn't quite get used to that, although he'd seen plenty of corpses. Those opened eyes always seemed to him to be silent witnesses.

"Can you hurry the drug report from Richmond?" Cooper mentioned the location of forensic research.

"It's Christmas. No one will be in a hurry, but, Sheriff, you can try to prod them a wee bit." Dr. Gibson's curiosity rose higher as he considered again the clean cut at the throat.

Rick crossed his arms over his chest. "Used a sharp blade."

"Yes, no ragged edge. The wound is quite neat and clean."

Cooper flipped her notebook shut for a moment. "No struggle. Drugs unknown at this point. Either he knew his assailant or the killer snuck up on him."

"Definite possibility." Dr. Gibson started to hum as he worked.

Rick understood how methodical most coroners were, especially Dr. Gibson. "I don't want to interrupt your procedure, but I am curious."

"I appreciate that," Dr. Gibson answered as he continued his exam.

"I'm curious, too. Seems to me that type of

cut had to be made by someone who knew what they were doing." Cooper was always fascinated by murder.

"Takes work and skill, which you know. If you pull the head back, it's easier to cut the jugular."

"Dr. Gibson, we'll leave you to it, and I thank you for coming down here at night," Rick said.

The old pathologist smiled. "House full of grandchildren. I needed the quiet."

After bidding the good doctor good-bye, the two work partners and friends drove to headquarters. Cooper followed Rick into his office, where he shut the door.

"Search back ten years to see if there's been any killing of priests, nuns, monks."

"Right."

"Are you sure you want extra duty over Christmas?"

She nodded in the affirmative. "My holiday will start New Year's Eve, when Lorenzo visits." She mentioned her boyfriend, whom she had met in the fall and was now home in Nicaragua. The romance was budding.

He looked at the large wall clock. "How'd it get to be two?"

"The earth just keeps revolving on its axis." She smiled, feeling ragged.

"Hey, go home. Get a good night's sleep. I

will, too. You know, sometimes if I give myself a problem to solve before I go to sleep, I wake up with the answer. Try it."

"I will."

"One more thing. See if you can keep Harry out of this. Bad enough she and Fair found the body." He rubbed his palm on his forehead as if to banish cares.

"Boss, I'll try, but don't hold your breath."

He laughed. Cooper left.

Rick did not take his own advice. He started searching for similar cases, even though he'd assigned the task to Cooper.

The phone rang at three-thirty.

Dr. Gibson's light voice was on the line. "Figured you'd be up. Sheriff, I found a curious thing in his mouth. Under his tongue there was an ancient Greek coin, an obol."

Rick, not having read much Greek mythology, blurted out, "What the hell could that mean?"

"Oh, the meaning is quite clear, Sheriff. He needed an obol to give to Charon, who pilots the dead across the River Styx to the underworld. If he doesn't have the coin, he wanders in limbo, a cruel fate."

"That is odd. He's murdered, but the killer wants him in the underworld."

"Not quite so odd, Sheriff. For one thing, it's a slap at his proclaimed Christianity. The killer is paying homage to the old gods. The other thing is, there may be someone waiting for him on the other side. Someone who will do even more damage."

Rick hung up the phone, knowing he needed sleep or a drink or both.

6

Tuesday, December 16. A light snow covered the tops of the Blue Ridge Mountains, but only a few swirling flakes traveled to the valley below. Still, those glistening rounded mountains, once the largest peaks in the world, looked perfect when the sun came out.

Susan drove Harry and herself in her Audi station wagon, a purchase she had never regretted. In the backseat, along with Christmas packages and a large fuzzy rug, sat Mrs. Murphy, Tucker, Pewter, and Owen, Susan's corgi and full brother to Tucker. When Susan's kids, now in college, reached the stage where she became a taxi, her corgi breeding fell by the wayside. She hoped to pick it back up, since it fascinated her.

"If I hear one more Christmas carol, I'm going to scream," Susan grumbled.

"Scream what?" Harry loved to tease Susan.

"How about, 'Jesus was born in March, why are we celebrating in December?' That ought to get their knickers in a knot."

"You know why as well as I do. We sat through six years of Latin. Too bad we didn't go to the same college. I kept on and you didn't."

Harry referred to the fact that the Roman winter-solstice festival, Saturnalia, was so popular the Christians couldn't dislodge it. Since they lacked a winter festival, they fudged on Jesus's birth, killing two birds with one stone.

"Ah, yes, Latin. I switched to French so I could order French food cooked by American chefs who pretend to know what they're doing." She braked as a Kia pulled out in front of her, the young man behind the wheel yakking away on a cell phone so tiny it was a wonder he could find it much less press in phone numbers.

"Ever notice that the people who take the most chances in the world are always in cheap cars?"

"No." Susan switched back to French cooking. "Actually there are some extraordinary French chefs now. I mean Americans who can cook."

"All men. If a man cooks, he's a chef. If a

woman cooks, she's a cook."

"Harry, you're being ever so slightly argumentative."

"Me?" Harry responded with mock surprise. "You, lovie."

Harry stared out the window at the jam-packed lot to Barracks Road Shopping Center. "Can't get Christopher out of my mind. Such a waste for him to die."

"When you called me, I couldn't believe it. We'd just been talking about him." Susan sighed as she began the hunt for a parking space. "Obviously no one has come forward to lay claim to the deed."

Harry smirked slightly. "Coop's keeping something from me. I can always tell."

"Harry, she can't tell you everything."

Harry shifted in her seat. "I know, but it drives me crazy."

"Not a far putt," Susan, a good golfer, teased her.

"She did tell me one thing this morning when I talked to her. Christopher had an obol under his tongue."

Susan, after the years of high school Latin and hearing about the myths, knew what that meant. "Aha. My parking karma is working." She slid into the space, popped the car in park, cut the motor. They sat still for a minute. "An obol for the ferryman. Some kind of symbolism, apparently."

"It's just so odd, but at least we have an educated killer."

"It is odd."

Harry shook her head. "He's fired up my curiosity."

"God help us," Pewter piped up.

"She gets these notions and we have to bail her out," Mrs. Murphy agreed.

"Then she gets my mother in trouble," Owen said.

"Look at it this way. No one is bored." Tucker had long ago resigned herself to Harry's curiosity.

"You all stay here." Harry had visions of returning to the Audi to find the interior shredded.

"I want to go with you," Tucker whined.

"Brownnoser," Pewter said with disdain.

"Oh, shut up, fatty."

The gray cat, giving her best Cheshire cat smile, purred maliciously. *"Hey, I'm not the one with my nose in the litter box, eating cat poop."*

"That's low." Owen blinked.

"Low, but true." Pewter, satisfied with the turn of conversation, snuggled farther down in the rug next to Mrs. Murphy.

"Pay her no mind, Tucker. Cats stick to-

gether." Owen leaned next to Tucker, who hoped she'd find a way to get even with Pewter.

Susan and Harry walked into the elegant framing shop called Buchanan and Kiguel.

Shirley Franklin, the good-looking and artistic lady behind the counter, peered over the customers' heads and called out, "How are you? Good to see you."

"Surviving the helladays," Harry quipped.

People laughed. Shirley was handing out wrapped custom-framed jobs. The finished work was lined up in special bins so it wouldn't fall over.

"The obol." Susan had noticed a pretty print of Aphrodite. "Pagan."

"I know that, you twit," Harry said softly.

"Maybe it means Brother Christopher was a fake."

Harry's expression changed as she turned to look Susan full in the face. "Hadn't thought of that."

"Or it's all about money. His scandal was about money." Susan's curiosity now ran as high as Harry's.

"Or both."

Back at the sheriff's headquarters, Cooper was glued to the computer screen, happy not to be on patrol today. The long night without much sleep had worn her down. A law-enforcement officer can't afford to miss things or be physically slowed down. Too much can happen, and it always happens fast.

Rick had given a statement to the media that morning. The phones sounded like a beehive, one buzz after the other.

He walked over and leaned over her shoulder. "They're coming out of the woodwork, these media wonders." The side of his mouth curled up slightly. "Didn't tell them about the obol."

"Yeah. I've been thinking about that. Don't even know where to look. I did tell Harry."

"She know any more than Dr. Gibson?" Rick inquired.

"No, but she said she'd review her old college texts."

"Least that keeps her out of our way."

"You think this murder has anything to do with Christmas?"

"Who knows? I'd like a little hard evidence. Check the airlines into Charlottesville to see if any passengers came in from Phoenix, Arizona."

"Will do."

"Grasping at straws," he acknowledged.

"But sometimes a loose, wide net does catch some fish."

7

The Queen of Crozet, elegant even in her barn clothes, watched as Fair took X-rays of her filly's right cannon bone.

Big Mim Sanburne adjusted her red cashmere scarf around her neck, wiggled her fingers in her cashmere-lined gloves. "Adolescence."

Although small, Big Mim was so called because her daughter was Little Mim.

Paul de Silva, Big Mim's trainer, looked on as Fair set up the plates and positioned the portable machine.

"She's a naughty girl." Fair stepped back, as did the other two, and he pressed the button on the long cord of the X-ray machine.

Fair wore lead-lined gloves. Any medical person, whether dental, vet, or human, needed to be prudent concerning X-ray equipment. No need to wind up glowing in the dark.

Paul crossed his arms over his chest.

"Least we know she can jump."

Big Mim found his light Spanish accent pleasing. The cadence, more singsong than English, enlivened his sentences. Then, too, he was a handsome young man, with jet-black hair, thin sideburns longer than most, and a tiny tuft of black hair under his lower lip. He was engaged to Mim's architect, Tazio Chappars. Big Mim took credit for getting them together. There was just enough truth in this so no one argued with her.

No one argued with her anyway, except for her late mother's sister, Aunt Tally, and her daughter, Little Mim. Little Mim's disagreements proved less vocal than the soon-to-be centenarian.

"Okay, last one." Fair positioned the machine again.

Mim looked outside the closed barn doors, which had big windows that allowed in a lot of light, as did the continuous skylight running on both sides of the roof seam. "Coming down now."

"Sure is." Fair clicked the photo. "We need the snow."

"Not much last winter," Paul agreed.

"There are so many people drawing off the water table now in Albemarle County that we're all going to be in trouble in a decade or even less." Big Mim and her husband, the mayor of Crozet, were particularly concerned about the environment.

"All over. The human animal will suck this planet dry." Fair carefully put the plates in a special pouch. "Mim, I'm ninety-nine percent sure she's popped a splint. I'll know more after I examine the X-rays, of course, but chances are it needs to reattach. She'll have a bit of jewelry there, so that's the end of strip classes."

Bone splints are not uncommon in horses. Usually the fragment does grow back to the main bone. Occasionally it doesn't, which causes the animal pain and then the vet has to surgically remove it. Like any surgery, it runs up the bills, and the recovery time bores the bejesus out of the horse, especially one as young and full of herself as Maggie, her barn name.

"Oh, well." Big Mim waved her hand. "I can live without strip classes. I leave those to Kenny Wheeler."

A strip class is a conformation class wherein the animal is stripped of tack. The judge bases his ribbons on the makeup of the animal, not performance. It's a beauty pageant. Kenny Wheeler, a famous horseman, won those classes all over the United States.

"He's got some good ones." Paul appreciated Mr. Wheeler's acumen.

"He has more money than God." Big Mim laughed.

"So do you," Fair teased her.

Most people were afraid of Big Mim and would never tease her, but Fair, knowing her since childhood, could get away with it. The fact that he was incredibly handsome helped.

"Maybe St. Peter. Not God." She laughed at herself, then told Paul, "How about putting her back in her stall? Let's not turn her out until we get the full report."

"Yes, madam." He touched his lad's cap and walked the bright filly back to her stall.

Fair carried the X-ray equipment and plates out to his truck. Like most vets, this was his mobile office. People had no idea how expensive it was for an equine vet to be properly equipped. The special truck cover alone cost $17,000.

Fair returned to Big Mim's large office. "Sit down." Big Mim motioned for Fair to sit by the fireplace.

The granary-oak floor shone. The sofa and chairs, covered in a dark tartan plaid, added color. A gorgeous painting, a hunt scene by Michael Lyne, hung over the fireplace. The walls, covered in framed photographs, bore testimony to Big Mim's successes in the show ring and the hunt field. She also had a photograph of Mary Pat Reines jumping over a fence in perfect, perfect form. Ever since she was young, this photo had prodded her on. She'd look at it and vow to ride more elegantly. Mary Pat had been Alicia Palmer's protector and lover when Alicia was in her twenties. Big Mim had never realized how a fierce rival pushes one to excellence until Mary Pat passed away. She missed her socially and truly missed her in the show ring. In some ways, the world had come full circle. Big Mim struck terror in the hearts of younger competitors because she was as elegant over fences as Mary Pat had been. And Alicia had come home from Hollywood once again to be part of the community.

"Fire feels good. Nothing quite like it, the hardwood odor, the flickering glow." Fair gratefully sank into the deep chair.

"In the old days, a small wood-burning stove would often be put in the tackroom. Not the safest solution. I remember the barn rats — what my father called 'the grooms' — huddled around the potbellied stove. There they'd be, wiping down the tack, breaking apart the bridles. In those days the bits were sewn into the bridles. Looks better than how it is today." She paused a moment, then smiled. "The vice of the old, recalling the golden years that correspond to one's youth."

"Your golden years never stopped." Fair complimented her, and in truth, Big Mim looked marvelous for a woman in her seventies.

"Now, now," she chided, but loved it. "Drink?"

"You know what, I'm going to fix myself a cup of tea. You stay seated."

"Then I'm not much of a hostess." She watched as he rose to go to the small kitchen area.

"You're the best hostess in the county and the best fund-raiser, too."

"The second-oldest profession." She put her feet up on a hassock after removing her paddock boots, which were slip-ons.

Fair turned on a faucet specially designed to produce water just a hair under boiling. "I keep meaning to ask you where you got this and then I forget."

"The boiling-water tap?"

"Yes."

"Most plumbing supplies have them."

"Think I'll get one for Harry for Christmas. No, I'll get two. One for the house and one for the barn."

"She'll like that."

"Got her a necklace to match the ring I

bought her when we were in Shelbyville."

"She'll like that, too. Harry is a very good-looking woman. It just takes a miracle to get her out of her jeans and into a dress."

"Actually, Big Mim, I like getting her out of her jeans."

They both laughed.

"I would imagine her Christmas spirit and yours are somewhat dimmed by what you saw. Rick called me, of course."

The sheriff knew to keep Big Mim in the pipeline. There would be hell to pay if he didn't; plus, her connections had helped him many a time. Big Mim knew everyone, and she had many, many favors she could call in.

Fair sipped his tea, a bracing Darjeeling. "No one likes coming upon a dead body. It upset Harry because she'd just talked to him that afternoon. She said he was committed to the order, to doing good in life."

"I expect most of the brothers are making up for some perceived or real sins. And some people are cut out for the contemplative life."

"I'm not one of them."

"Obviously not." She smiled.

"If Rick talked to you, then you know whoever slit his throat did so with skill and speed."

"Yes." She paused. "And Christopher gave no alarm."

"No."

"Strange. And no footprints in the snow?"

"The snow was mashed down," he replied.

"If the killer is smart, and I reckon he is, he could have walked backward in his footsteps until it was safe to turn around."

"Never thought of that." Fair paused a moment. "Harry thinks there will be more killings." He half-smiled. "You know Harry."

"Let's hope she's wrong, but the fact that this had to be well thought-out and fairly quickly executed — at the back of the tree farm, which was open to the public — suggests a killer with a good mind. You know what I mean: a smart person, however misshapen his moral code, with perhaps an assistant."

"Ah. Never thought about an assistant."

"The work would go more quickly." She stopped herself, then continued, "What I don't understand is why someone didn't hear them."

"The element of surprise, perhaps? Then again, what if he knew his killer? Sure would simplify the process."

"Yes." She folded her hands together.

"And the Christmas tree farm, like any business, has peak hours of activity. In this case, people would come in the largest numbers after work. Brother Sheldon was up front. He'd occupy them."

"Think Brother Sheldon was in on it?"

"No. He did seem genuinely distraught, and he passed out. I've never passed out. Must be a strange feeling."

"I did once, in Venice of all places. Felt a little weak and woozy. Next thing I remember is waking up with Big Jim picking me up and people speaking in Italian so fast I couldn't understand a word. It could be, just to play devil's advocate," she switched back to the primary subject, "that Brother Sheldon was acting or that he hadn't anticipated how the sight would affect him."

"The passing out was genuine. I really don't think he was part of the murder. Of course, Harry and I were there in the dark. We probably missed things. There was no sign of struggle, but there was blood all around the tree. I know I missed a lot."

"Anyone other than a law-enforcement officer would. And even they miss things sometimes."

"Funny thing, though. Harry says she doesn't want a tree now. I expect she'll change her mind. She'll see trees everywhere, so maybe the emotion will pass."

"I didn't know Christopher Hewitt. I knew

him as a child. After all, everyone sees everyone else, and he was close in age to Little Mim and you all, but I didn't know him. He wasn't part of your crowd. I knew what everyone else knew: the insider-trading scandal. He seemed mild enough. But then, perhaps successful criminals always do — the kind that steal millions, I mean."

"White-collar crime is so different from what I think of as lower forms of crime: assault and battery, murder, petty theft. Those crimes, I think, are committed by people with poor impulse control. Low normals, really." He used the expression for low-normal intelligence. "White-collar crimes demand intelligence, a bland exterior for the most part, and vigilance. Constant vigilance to cover your tracks." He thought a moment. "I suppose premeditated murder and large-scale robbery demand intelligence."

"Murder is easier to accomplish and remain undetected than television crime dramas acknowledge. Why do you think there's so much publicity when a murder is solved?"

Fair finished his tea. "Also fuels the illusion that you can't get away with murder, when you can."

"I wonder if the killer is reveling in the publicity. The greatest luxury in life is privacy."

"That it is." He smiled. "Another luxury is having your wife listen to you even if she's a trifle bored."

She smiled. "I doubt she finds you boring. But you know how she, um, becomes obsessed. If ever there was a person who shouldn't have seen the remains of Christopher Hewitt, that person is Harry."

As Big Mim and Fair chatted, Dr. Bryson Deeds was having lunch at Farmington Country Club with his lawyer and college friend, Bill Keelo, a man as high-powered in his way as Bryson was in his.

Seated at the next table was a group of eight who'd finished a game of platform tennis, which was played outside on a raised platform in a cage. They sweated so much the snow didn't bother them, but it finally got so slippery everyone had to stop. Each court hosted a foursome, mixed doubles. The exhilarating exercise put everyone in high spirits, as did the holidays. Anthony McKnight, president of a small but quite successful local bank, and Arnold Skaar, a retired stockbroker, were part of the group. Both men knew and had business relations with Bryson and Bill. Arnie was in everyone's good book because he still made them money during recessions, both mild and deep.

Bryson stabbed his salmon. "Spoke to Brother Morris this morning."

"Me, too. He's distraught." Bill noticed as Donald Hormisdas, another lawyer, passed their table and waved. "Faggot," Bill hissed.

Bryson ignored the slur on Donald, as he'd heard it so many times from Bill. "Apart from the emotional loss, Brother Morris is upset because Brother Christopher had such a good business mind."

"He certainly was persuasive. I'd worked as their lawyer for years at a reduced fee, and Christopher convinced me to do their work for free."

Bryson smiled slightly at Bill. "He could talk a dog off a meat wagon."

Aunt Tally entered the room, accompanied by her great-niece, Little Mim. As Tally passed each table, the gentlemen rose to greet her. For one thing, this displayed superb manners, something a fellow should consider if he wished to seduce a lady. Women noticed such things, just as most women could recall to the slightest detail what she wore the first time she met a man and what he wore last week to the basketball game. For another thing, Aunt Tally walked with a silver-headed cane. The silver head was in the graceful shape of a hound. If you didn't stand up and say something mildly fawning, Aunt Tally would whack you. Worse, she'd tell everyone you had the manners of a warthog. You were cooked.

"Aunt Tally, how lovely you look in your red and green." Bryson stood.

Bill, not to be outdone, lightly kissed her hand and said, "Aunt Tally, you look ravishing in any color." He turned his attentions to Little Mim. "Merry Christmas."

"Merry Christmas to you," Little Mim replied.

"Will you all be at St. Luke's Christmas party?" Aunt Tally lived for parties and the attendant gossip.

Bryson replied, "Both our wives are on the decorating committee. We'll be there."

Aunt Tally smiled as though their being at the party would be the most glorious thing.

"Damned thing, that mess at the Brothers of Love tree farm." Aunt Tally rapped her cane on the floor. "On the other hand, it does give people something to talk about. I'm sick of climatic observations." With that, she moved on to accept her obeisance at the table of people who'd just played platform tennis.

Little Mim, wearing a pair of gold dome earrings her husband had given her as one of his twelve days of Christmas presents, winked to the men as she hurried after Aunt Tally.

Tally's only concession to her advanced age was the cane, but the old girl could travel along with it at amazing speed.

The two men sat back down.

Bill asked, "Think there's anything we can do for the brothers?"

Bryson shook his head. "Not really. Just help them continue to do their work."

8

A murder such as Christopher Hewitt's would cause a storm of speculation in any community. As it was, Crozet elevated gossip to a new art form.

Cooper's phone rang with the usual people who felt compelled to inform her of their ideas about Christopher's murder. Not one scrap of evidence was transmitted. She listened patiently as she marveled at the human capacity for making pronouncements without a shred of research.

"Assaulted by theories," she had said of these calls to Rick, as he drove them up Afton Mountain. The trip revealed a beautiful view of the Rockfish Valley, which ran south of Route 64, parallel to the mountains.

"Me, too. Most of the ones I've been enduring insist this goes back to his bringing down people in Phoenix. It might, but he parked his ass in the slammer. Of course, a person bent on revenge for their money losses might not have had time to kill him before he was put in jail." He thought a moment. "Haven't had as many calls as usual with a murder. Christmas has given people more to think about than Christopher Hewitt, I guess."

"Biddy Doswell told me he was dispatched by aliens."

Rick laughed. "Land in a flying saucer, did they?"

Cooper shook her head. "No. These aliens are gnomes with mole feet and human hands. They dig up out of the earth. Gopher holes are their preferred exit, so we don't notice anything strange."

"A gnome with mole feet and human hands, and that's not strange."

"Biddy says we can't see them."

"That's convenient. The woman is all of twenty-five years old. Barking mad." He sighed as they neared the top of the mountain, where they'd be turning south on the Blue Ridge Parkway. "What's her theory about why they killed Christopher?"

Biddy had earned her name because she was the smallest of five children, a little biddy thing.

"They don't like red beards." Cooper shook her head in disbelief. "Red beards."

"It's more than we've got to go on." Rick

had a vision of every man with a red beard being killed.

"Her other helpful hint was that these gnomes like to have sex around the clock. They drink to excess, too." She rooted around in her bag for a cigarette. "Wonder if her idea is wish fulfillment?"

"Take one of mine." He pointed to a pack of Camels he pulled from the back of the visor.

She accepted the pack from him, taking a cigarette for herself and handing one to Rick. Fishing a sturdy Zippo from the glove compartment, she lit his cigarette while it was in his mouth and then lit hers. Each took a deep, grateful drag.

"Swore I wasn't going to get hooked, but I did." Cooper sighed.

"In our job it's drink, drugs, violence, or cigarettes. People haven't a clue the toll this kind of work takes on a person. I worry most about the guys who get addicted to violence. Sooner or later they cross the line, make the news, and all law-enforcement officers suffer. And in those big-city departments, they're bombarded. Je-sus." He drew out the name of Jesus. "We see enough right here in Albemarle County."

"We sure do. What gets me is when we see murdered children — fortunately, very few.

But we see a lot more abused children than anyone cares to admit. It's like the whole damned country has its head in the sand."

"Yeah." He wanted to kill people who harmed children, preferably with his bare hands. "Ownership. Think about it. Children have no rights. Their parents own them the same way they own a car. Ah, here we are."

"Before we deal with the brothers — do you mean that because children are chattel, owned, that people outside the family or the situation don't want to interfere?"

"Same as spousal abuse. People know, but they don't want to get involved. I can understand it, but, guess what, we do get involved. When that call comes, we don't have any choice. And family situations are the worst."

"Sure are. Well, let's visit this big happy family," Cooper said sarcastically, for she harbored a slight prejudice against aggressive do-gooders.

Brother George, in his mid-forties and with a trimmed gray beard, met them at the door. He ushered them into Brother Morris's office.

"Brother Morris will be with you in a minute. He's in the kitchen with Brother Howard."

No sooner were the words out of his mouth than the imposing figure of Brother

Morris swept through the door. As flamboyantly as Brother Morris entered, Brother George, an attractive man yet devoid of charisma, left discreetly.

"Sit down, please." He gracefully lowered his bulk into a large club chair with a cashmere shawl thrown over the back. Brother Morris pulled the shawl around his shoulders on the bitterly cold days, extra cold on the mountain's spine.

Cooper pulled out her stenographer's notebook, but before Rick could start, Brother Morris asked if they wanted a drink. They declined, although Cooper longed for a cup of hot coffee.

"Brother Morris, I know this is a very difficult time for you and the order, but I need to ask you a few questions."

"Of course. None of us will be completely free of doubt until the murderer is found. Odd, isn't it, that one can be at peace but not at rest, so to speak?"

"Yes, it is." Rick knew what Brother Morris meant. "I don't want to offend you by these questions, but it is very important that you be forthcoming. Our ability to solve this case early in many ways depends on you."

"I don't see how it can, but I will be forthcoming, as you say. That's a very Southern way to say, 'Tell the truth.' "

Rick half-smiled. "Is there anyone in your order who has ever threatened Brother Christopher?"

"No."

"Anyone who disliked him?"

"He was so easygoing. At times Brother Sheldon would get peeved. I don't say he disliked Brother Christopher, because he didn't, but he would get out of sorts. Brother Sheldon is quite the stickler for detail, and Brother Christopher was not, not in the least. The money from the Christmas trees would be in the desk drawer down there in the trailer. No tags, no records of who bought what so we could cultivate friendships. Used to drive Brother Sheldon mad as he'd try to figure out the money."

"Do you think Brother Christopher was stealing from the order?"

"No. He just wasn't detail-oriented." Brother Morris frowned slightly. "Insider trading isn't exactly stealing, but I know Brother Christopher repented of his misdeeds. He also repented worshipping Mammon."

"A national affliction," Rick smoothly said.

"I was guilty of it. That and pride." Brother Morris warmed to his subject. "But I saw the light — literally, I saw the light — and I found my true calling. You will meet few men happier than myself."

"You are most fortunate." Rick waited a beat. "Who is the order's treasurer?"

"Brother Luther. By the way, Officer Doak was very kind to Brother Sheldon. Sorry, I got off track. Well, what I was about to add is that Brother Luther is a worrywart. Then again, most treasurers are. We get by. The sale of the Christmas trees is a large part of our annual income." He drummed his fingers on his knee. "May we open for business soon?"

"Our team should be out by four this afternoon. I see no reason why you can't open. People's love of the ghoulish may even increase business." Rick wanted to see Brother Morris's reaction.

Brother Morris replied, "That's the premise behind horror movies, I think — to watch the fearful deed from a safe distance. Of course, in Brother Christopher's case, who is to say what is a safe distance?"

"I don't know," Rick honestly answered. "Brother Morris, what are the vows of your order?"

"Chastity, poverty, and obedience. We're all human. Each man struggles with his vows — some men more than others, some vows more than others. But everyone tries."

"Do you punish a brother if he breaks a vow?"

Brother Morris smoothly replied, "We do not judge. That doesn't mean I don't assign extra chores or encourage more prayer."

"Did Brother Christopher break his vows?"

"No. Not that I know of. Why?" For the first time Brother Morris displayed how intrigued he really was.

"In breaking a vow he may have upset someone else."

"Another brother?"

Rick replied, "Possibly. But it could have been someone outside the order."

Brother Morris cast his eyes down at the faded Persian rug. "Did he suffer?"

"Physically, no. Now, if he knew his killer, at the last moment he might have been shocked."

"I hate to think of it." Brother Morris's voice was low.

"Could he have had an affair with any women in the area?"

"I doubt it. The usual signs — going off the grounds, staying out on some nights, being preoccupied — Brother Christopher never acted like that. This isn't to say that he couldn't have hidden it, but I don't think he did."

"I would imagine that celibacy is a trial."

"You know, that depends on a man's experiences in life, his age, and his drive. Some people don't have a strong sex drive."

"Yes." Rick pressed on. "Has there ever been money missing from the treasury?"

"No. Brother Luther is a ferocious watchdog."

"Do you know Greek mythology?" Rick asked.

"Thanks to opera I know more Norse mythology. Why?"

"An obol was found under Brother Christopher's tongue."

This puzzled Brother Morris, disturbed him slightly. "Whatever could that signify?"

"I was hoping you'd know."

The rest of the questioning continued in this vein until, frustrated by their lack of progress, Rick and Cooper left.

9

Fascinated by the obol under the tongue, Harry called the classics departments at the University of Virginia, William & Mary, and Duke, where she had friends who taught the early historians.

Given the thousands of years that the myths had persisted, slight variations existed concerning Charon. The standard version of him as a somewhat disreputable ferryman held sway. If you didn't press an obol into his palm, you'd be stuck on the shores until you could beg, borrow, or steal the small sum. Given that one was dead, this could prove difficult, so the families of the deceased took great care to include the fare with the corpse. Since Greeks often carried small coins under their tongues — unthinkable with today's money — it was natural to put an obol under the tongue as well.

Nothing new transpired with her phone calls. Harry then called a local coin dealer,

Morton Nadal, and was surprised to find a very upset man on the line.

"Why are you asking me about the obols?" he demanded.

"Uh, well, curiosity." The small detail had not yet found its way into the ever-intrusive media.

"Are you in on it?"

"Sir, in on what?"

"You're the third person to call me about my obols. I have coins from Alexandria, Athens, Corinth, but it's all obols."

"I'm sorry to bother you."

"What did you say your name was again?"

"Mrs. Fair Haristeen. I live in Crozet."

"Hold on a moment." After a brief interlude he again spoke: "Well, that's a real name, but it may not be yours. The other two people gave fake names, although I didn't check when they first called."

"Again, Mr. Nadal, I'm sorry. I only wanted to know if you'd sold any."

"Not a one. Some were stolen the night before last, I think, but I didn't find out until today." Before she could say anything, he added, his voice raised, "I'm meticulous, and no one broke in to the front of the house where I keep my collection."

"How do you think they were stolen?"

"What's it to you?"

"I'm sorry, Mr. Nadal. I can see I'm a bother. I assume you called the sheriff."

"Did." He hung up the phone.

Harry then called Cooper, relaying the conversation.

"He's a piece of work and looks just like you think he would — a large ant with glasses." Cooper exhaled. "Two people went into his house, a woman and a man. He gave a lax description, only that they were more young than old, the man distracted him, the woman took the obols."

"Why didn't he find it out then?"

"She'd put fake coins in their place — same size, anyway — and I guess he was in a hurry. I don't know. He's a weird little thing and so excitable."

"Nothing useful?"

"Only that the man was largish, had a mustache and a big laugh."

"Anything else?"

"Three obols were stolen."

"Three?"

"Three."

10

"Who died and made you God?" Pewter, tail moving slightly, spit at Tucker.

"Jealous." Tucker smiled, then walked away from the angry gray cat.

Tucker had stayed with Harry as Harry made all the phone calls. The cats had been in the barn.

Mrs. Murphy, irritated herself, prudently did not insult the corgi. *"If you piss her off, she'll never tell."*

Pewter, upset though she was with the idea that a mere dog could consider herself superior to a cat, hated the idea of being uninformed even more. An argument could be made that the rotund kitty lived for gossip. Pewter thought of it as news.

"You're right." Pewter's admission nearly floored the tiger cat. *"But I'm not going to make it up to her. You can do that."*

Sighing deeply, Mrs. Murphy walked after Tucker, who had repaired to the living room

to flop in front of the fireplace.

Harry and Fair sat at opposite ends of the large sofa, a throw over their legs, slippers on the floor, each reading a book.

The aroma of burning wood pleased Mrs. Murphy, so long as the smoke didn't invade her eyes. She sat next to the dog.

Tucker lifted her head. *"Too bad we couldn't have gone to the coin dealer. We pick up things the humans might miss."*

"Mother isn't leaving a stone unturned about the ancient coins." Mrs. Murphy settled down next to the dog, who had informed her of the conversations.

"Pewter still having a cow?" The dog laughed, which came out as little wind puffs.

"Given her state, I think she's having a water buffalo." Mrs. Murphy kneaded the rug.

"May they be happy together."

This made Mrs. Murphy laugh so loudly that Harry and Fair looked up from their books and started laughing.

Pewter, in the kitchen, heard it all and was doubly furious. *"You're talking about me. I know it!"*

"Yes, we are," Tucker called out.

Pewter shot out of the kitchen, into the living room. Upon reaching Tucker, she puffed up and jumped sideways.

Mrs. Murphy dryly commented, *"You've scared Tucker half to death."*

"Serves her right." Pewter flounced next to Mrs. Murphy.

"We weren't really talking about you," Tucker fibbed.

This disappointed Pewter, who felt she was the center of the universe.

Quickly changing the subject, Tucker said, *"Maybe whoever put the coin under Christopher's tongue is crazy. There's no logic to it."*

"Maybe. Maybe it's camouflage," Mrs. Murphy said.

Pewter gave up her anger to curiosity. *"Why do you say that?"*

"Humans pretend they're crazy to cover up bad things. They get away with it, too. At least, I think they do."

Tucker, alert now, roused herself to sit up. *"Isn't it odd how people miss so much about one another? I can understand that they can't smell emotions — just the sweat of fear, for instance — but they listen to what people say instead of watching them."*

"Maybe they don't want to know." Pewter blinked as an ember crackled and flew up against the fire screen.

Mrs. Murphy, the end of her tail swishing slightly, remarked, *"Could be. Then again, theft, graft, political violence — that's human behavior. Corruption"* — she shrugged — *"just the way they do business, a lot of them, anyway, and it's always the ones who make the most fuss about morals. Humans rarely kill one another over corruption or political ideas short of revolution. When they kill, it's usually personal. When I think about Christopher Hewitt being killed, I try to find that link to another human. Something close."*

"Hmm." Pewter watched Harry take her yellow highlighter to run over something in her book. *"But isn't that the thing about monks: they aren't close. They've withdrawn from the world, pretty much."*

Tucker lifted her head. *"Maybe. Maybe not."*

Pewter, listening intently to what Mrs. Murphy just said, replied, *"I resent getting involved in human messes. I don't give a fig about Christopher Hewitt. Harry drags us in."*

As the animals chatted, Harry's cell rang. "Hello."

Brother Morris answered, "Hello, Harry, Brother Morris here. In all our grief and upset over our loss, I forgot your sorrow. After all, you and Fair knew Brother Christopher longer than any of us. I am sorry you found him. I'm so sorry you've had to see a high school friend like that."

Harry responded, "Thank you. We will all miss him." She then asked, "How are you doing? I know this is hard for you."

A pause followed this question. "It takes some time for it to sink in. I try to remember that God loves us all, even killers. I try not to hate, to judge the sin and not the sinner, but at this moment I am not successful. I'd like to get my hands on this, this —" He sputtered because he couldn't find the right word.

"That's only natural."

"Well, I don't mean to burden you with my feelings."

"I asked. If we're true Christians, then am I not my brother's keeper?"

Another long pause followed. "Yes, Harry, you are. Thank you for reminding me."

"Anything I can do for you?"

"Yes. We're singing at St. Luke's Christmas party, which you know. I look forward to it, but I've lost my pitch pipe. Do you have one? It would save a trip down the mountain."

"I'll get one. We're going to have a huge crowd because you're singing."

"That's very flattering."

"How often do we hear a Met star?" Harry named the New York opera house where Brother Morris enjoyed his first taste of fame.

"Again, that's very flattering, but my gift is useless if it's not in God's service."

Harry kept her deepest religious thoughts to herself. She never quite trusted those who flaunted theirs. But Brother Morris was a monk, so perhaps his protestations of faith weren't as offensive as if coming from a layperson. Still, it made her want to take a step back.

Instead, she said, "What's wonderful, Brother Morris, is that everyone has some God-given talent. At least, I hope so." She paused a moment and her humor took over. "Some people's talent is to make the rest of us miserable. That way we realize how lucky we are when they aren't around and that we're not that kind of person. See, nothing is wasted."

He chuckled. "Harry, you're incorrigible. You know that talent was a form of money during Roman times. It's interesting that a special skill demanded talent, more money. Over time we get talent in its modern form."

"Took Latin."

"Lucky you. When they removed Latin from the schools and as a requirement to get into college, they assigned generations to ignorance. Those who don't know the past are doomed to repeat it, and those who don't know Latin don't know the past. They don't even know their own language."

"I appreciate that, but at the time our high school Latin teacher was such a dragon. Hated every minute of it. Do you know we had to sing 'I Wonder Who's Kissing Her Now' in Latin?"

He laughed. "I take it your Latin teacher was elderly."

"Yes. She was pickled in high-grade bourbon, but she never let a declension slip." Harry laughed, too. "Do you need the pitch pipe before the party? Sorry, Brother Morris, I do that all the time, just switch from one subject to another. I mean, do you need me to run the pitch pipe up to you tomorrow?"

"No, I can do without. If you'd be so kind as to give it to me when we arrive at St. Luke's, that would be sufficient."

"Will do."

"You and Fair are in our prayers."

They said their good-byes. Harry hit the end button on her cell and said to Fair, "Brother Morris needs a pitch pipe."

"Get it back from him after the party and put it on eBay. You'll make a bundle."

Harry smiled at him. "Good idea, but I don't think I'll ask for it back. And he wanted to talk about Christopher, but he wasn't maudlin. He was solicitous about us since we knew Christopher from high school. Very kind of him, really."

11

On Thursday, December 18, the temperature plunged into the mid-twenties, quite cold by Virginia standards. A swirl of snow heightened the sense that it truly was Christmas. Try as she might, Harry couldn't get into the spirit. She turned off the Christmas carols on the radio as she drove. They irritated her, and she usually enjoyed them.

Harry thought about body language. How the body told the truth, whether it was Tucker's extra alertness and sweet expression when the biscuit tin was opened or whether it was Fair swearing he wasn't exhausted when she could see his six-foot-five-inch frame sagging from the hard physical work an equine vet must perform. The hours were unpredictable. A call would come in at three in the morning. He'd jump out of bed, get in his truck, and drive. She'd drag herself out of bed and make him a thermos of coffee in the time it took him to put on his flannel-lined coveralls. One of her unspoken fears was that he'd be so dead-tired he'd drive off the road. The last of foaling season ended in July, so by that time things would calm down. Then they'd both say a prayer of gratitude.

Drivers on Route 250 were usually more sensible than those on the interstate, who would fly along above the speed limit in wretched weather. The old Three Chopt Road, one branch of which was Route 250, was more used by locals and proved safer in the snow.

At the top of Afton Mountain, she swung right, the remnants of an old Howard Johnson hotel still in pathetic evidence. She slowly drove down the steep grade into Waynesboro. Charlottesville, especially now during the holidays, was strangled with traffic. She loathed it. So many outsiders now lived in Albemarle County, and they brought their ways with them, which included rudeness behind the wheel of a vehicle. One would hope the Virginia Way would rub off on the heathens, but it appeared to be going the other way 'round. People she knew would lean on the horn, give someone the finger while cussing a blue streak. She flat-out hated it.

The additional appeal of Waynesboro, a

modest town with no pretensions, was that prices were cheaper than in Charlottesville, the land of the truly rich and famous. Not that she had anything against rich and famous people, except for one thing: their presence drove prices ever upward.

A little music store squatted just over the bridge at the base of Main Street. She parked by the curb, feeling lucky to get a space, dashed in, and bought three pitch pipes: one for Brother Morris, one for St. Luke's, and one for herself. Funny, Morris thought he'd have to go down the mountain in bad weather. Clearly he didn't shop much in Waynesboro. Harry was a good driver. She enjoyed this little foray.

Mrs. Murphy, Pewter, and Tucker had snuggled up on the sheepskin throw on the truck bench. The cab of the old 1978 F-150 was warm, but if the engine wasn't on, it cooled fast enough.

"*She's got that look,*" Mrs. Murphy announced.

"*Are you surprised?*" Pewter sarcastically snorted.

"*No,*" the tiger replied. "*I'm surprised that it took her this long to get it.*"

"*She was upset at seeing the body,*" Tucker sagely noted. "*You know Mom, she doesn't show much emotion, but the murder affected her. Then, too, I think emotions are closer to the surface around Christmas. She's full of memories."*

"Better pray to the Great Cat in the Sky, because she's back to her old self," Mrs. Murphy said. *"The worst part of it is, she has no clues."*

"What's so bad about that?" Pewter wondered.

"She'll blunder into something or set someone off. If she had even a hint of what's going on, I'd feel better." The tiger cat snuggled closer to Tucker.

"Me, too." Tucker sighed.

Harry returned to the truck and drove up Main Street, turning left at the light where Burger King, McDonald's, Rite Aid, and a BP station clustered. Traffic proved heavier now. She finally turned into the parking lot of Martin's, a good supermarket. Fortunately, she didn't have a lot of shopping, but she never looked forward to any kind of shopping.

Once inside, she grabbed a cart and headed for produce. She threw in carrots and apples — for the horses as well as for herself — varieties of lettuce and oranges, then she raced to the meat department.

She slowed when she noticed Brother Speed and Bryson Deeds at the far end of the meat section. Putting her new vow into practice, she studied their body language. They looked like two people who knew each other very well. She racked her brain to think how these two disparate souls would know each other. Bryson, not a horseman, couldn't even be induced to attend the steeplechase races, a social event above and beyond flat racing at Colonial Downs. She knew Bryson treated the brothers pro bono. She hoped Brother Speed didn't have heart problems, although the handsome jockey appeared the picture of health. Given that they both worked at the hospice, they'd had plenty of opportunity to take each other's measure.

Fascinated, she watched these two as they leaned toward each other in deep conversation.

She remembered Brother Speed's compact body when he was in racing silks. His monk's robe covered up everything.

She wouldn't have minded squeezing Brother Speed's buns back in his racing days, not that she wanted to go to bed with him, but he was once so cute. It occurred to her at that very moment that she lived in a culture where most forms of touching were taboo. She wondered what it would be like to live in a culture where people didn't have mental body armor.

Bryson's body displayed the signs of a middle-aged man. Well fed. A potbelly sagged over his pants. Not bad, but no six-pack, that was for sure. He was a tad under six feet, reasonably well built. Had he been fit he would have been better-looking. His face's strong features gave him a commanding look. His dark brown eyes were deep-set. His hair, receding, showed signs of gray at the temples. The color, also a dark brown, suited his complexion, somewhat olive. She could see his wedding ring, plus another ring on the pinky of his right hand, probably a family crest. She hadn't noticed it before. An expensive Rolex Submariner watch, gold with a blue bezel, flashed just enough money spent that an observant person would take that into account. Plus, Bryson gave off the air of a man accustomed to getting his way, not unusual in a doctor.

Brother Speed stepped aside as an elderly man pushing a half-full cart careened dangerously close. When he did so, he saw Harry. His face registered pleasure at her presence, then he smiled, said something to Bryson, and the two men walked toward her.

"Christmas dinner?" Bryson asked. "I don't see the goose."

"Maybe you're looking at her," Harry

joked. "I've been called a silly goose."

"Not you." Brother Speed smiled again, for he liked Harry above and beyond the fact that she was a true horsewoman, as opposed to just being a rider.

"You're too kind. You all doing the same thing I am?"

"Racquel gave me a short list and told me that I had to stop at Martin's on the way back from Augusta Medical. Only Martin's will do." He showed Harry the list. "I think I can get this stuff, but I'm not sure about the plum pudding."

"If they don't have it, try Foods of All Nations, if you can even get near it."

"That's the truth," Bryson commented.

"Whole Foods." Brother Speed mentioned another upscale market.

"I never knew you were interested in food." Harry recognized the sacrifices jockeys made.

"I'm not. Brother Morris is, and he often gives me the shopping job because Brother Howard can't be trusted not to dip into the bags on the way home."

"Come to think of it, what a wise decision." Harry laughed, for Brother Howard was as round as he was tall.

"We're having a service tomorrow, just among the brothers, and Brother Morris wants the reception to be a feast of celebration, to remember Brother Christopher's remarkable journey."

Bryson's dark eyebrows came together for a moment. "Harry, is his family doing anything? Haven't heard a peep, but under the circumstances it may take them more time."

"Oh, Bryson, that's one of the things that makes this so sad. His family disowned him when the scandal broke in Phoenix." She looked at Brother Speed. "I don't know if he ever talked about it." When Brother Speed shook his head, she continued. "His father, president of a bank that has been gobbled up like most of them, just turned his back on him. In a way I can understand it, because Mr. Hewitt believed passionately that anyone who dealt in money, whether a banker or a broker, had to be above reproach. Two years after the scandal, Christopher's mother died. He was in jail, and his father didn't even send him an obituary. He found out when Reverend Jones sent one to him after trying to persuade the old man to heal the wound with his son, given their mutual deep loss."

"Poor fellow," Bryson, a man of high feeling as well as self-regard, said.

"I had no idea." Brother Speed shook his head. "Occasionally, Brother Christopher spoke of his ex-wife. A trophy wife, as near as I could tell, and when times got hard, she sailed on."

"That's about it," Harry said. "You two are coming to the St. Luke's party. I'll see you there. I want to knock this out in case the mountain gets worse."

"Good idea." Bryson looked at Brother Speed, then clapped him on the back and rolled his cart down the bread aisle.

"Harry, this spring I'd like to come out and see your yearlings. You and Alicia Palmer keep the old bloodlines going."

"Sure. Love to have you."

Brother Speed then headed toward produce.

While Harry was in the grocery, Racquel was visiting Aunt Phillipa.

Her oxygen bag, with a tube in her nose, helped the old lady breathe. She could speak without gasping.

"Let it be," Aunt Phillipa advised.

"You're right. I'm letting little things get under my skin."

"No man is worth this much worry." Aunt Phillipa stopped. "You're his wife. If he sleeps around, you still have the power. Remember that."

"Yes, Aunt Phillipa."

"You know, I'd kill for a cigarette, but I'd blow us all up."

"Not a good idea." Racquel laughed, for she did love her old feisty aunt.

Bill Keelo walked into the private room. "Merry Christmas."

"What a beautiful amaryllis."

"I remembered that you liked the white." Bill's tie — little Santa Claus figures against a green background — gave him a seasonal air.

"You remembered correctly."

Alex Corbett stuck his head in the room. "Two good-looking women."

"What are you doing here?" Racquel wondered.

"Bill does the hospice's tax work. I'm looking for a larger piece of land down here for them."

"No kidding." Racquel was surprised.

"You can depend on dying. When the boomers start to go, it will be a bonanza." Aunt Phillipa put on her glasses to better admire the amaryllis.

"Guess so," Bill agreed.

"Shame about Brother Christopher." Aunt Phillipa was focused on dying. "He didn't work here as much as the others, but he was a bright penny."

"Yes, he was," Alex concurred. "We're all

upset. Bryson, too." He nodded to Racquel.

"He did mention it was a loss. I think doctors harden themselves to the inevitable. Although Brother Christopher's inevitable came early."

"In which case," Aunt Phillipa honestly stated, "I have nothing to complain about."

12

Two white five-foot tapers stood vigil next to the altar, the light from their flames making the huge brass stands glow. Two smaller white candles graced the altar, and the sconces on the wall flickered with candles. The monastery, built before electricity, had sconces throughout all the halls, as well.

Life may not have been easier before electricity, but people certainly looked better in candles' glow.

The service for Brother Christopher, conducted with dignity, left all the brothers in tears, most especially Brother Sheldon. Brother Ed, standing next to Brother Howard during the service, noted that Brother Sheldon could weep buckets at a sentimental commercial. His whisper brought a stare from Brother Luther, who was in charge of the service.

Brother Morris sang "Ave Maria," a cappella. The beauty of his voice filled the chapel as the flames leapt higher.

Brother Howard's reception, also by candelight, allowed the men the chance to tell Brother Christopher stories, citing his peculiarities such as a fondness for Sour Balls. Such tiny things helped soothe the shock, the loss.

Brother Speed watched as the others drank wine donated by Kluge Estate Winery and Vineyard.

"Miss it?" Brother Luther bluntly asked.

"Sure." Brother Speed nodded. "But drink and drugs gave me a ticket to hell. Can't do it."

"Takes a lot of discipline," Brother Luther complimented him.

"Not if you know it's going to kill you," Brother Speed replied.

"I never thought of that."

"You never had to."

"You're right. My journey was different. Bland. Boring even." He looked Brother Speed in the eye. "All paths lead to God, even ones as different as ours."

"Indeed, Brother Luther, indeed."

Brother Sheldon, sitting in a straight-backed chair, tears flowing as freely as the wine, stiffened up as Brother Morris and Brother George came over.

"He is with God," Brother George, a note

of unctuousness in his voice, said.

Brother Sheldon may have been a candidate for the American Academy of Dramatic Arts, given his ability to change his emotions at breakneck pace, but he knew when he was being patronized. "Thank you, Brother."

"We'll all miss him. He was good with the patients, good with those who came to visit them." Brother Morris sighed. "But as Brother George said, he is with God, and no matter how terrible the end of his mortal life, he is now rejoicing."

"I'll remember that," Brother Sheldon said dryly.

He believed it, but they hadn't seen Brother Christopher's body. He had. Awful though that was, he did have special status because of it.

"I'd like you to do something." Brother George leaned over.

Brother Sheldon looked up. "Yes."

"Take a beautiful Christmas tree to Harry Haristeen. It seems the least we can do."

Brother Sheldon brightened. "I will. When would you like me to deliver it?"

"Tomorrow." Brother Morris stepped in. "I know she'll be pleased to see you up and about, so to speak."

"I like Harry," Brother Sheldon said.

"We all like Harry." Brother Morris

smiled. "She's a straight shooter."

"Anyone ever see her in a dress?" Brother George wondered.

"Where did that come from?" Brother Morris was amused.

"I don't know. I've only seen her in jeans. I like to see women . . . you know." His hands made a curving motion.

"I expect she'll wear a dress to the St. Luke's Christmas party." Brother Morris smiled. "And you know, Alicia Palmer and BoomBoom Craycroft will be there, too. They're more your type, I think, Brother George."

Brother George laughed at himself. "Oh, those days are long gone, but I can dream. A man's still a man."

The two left Brother Sheldon, who now received Brother Ed and Brother Speed. The waterworks turned on again.

As the head of the order and his second in command walked toward the door, Brother George whispered in a low voice, "I really am going to miss Brother Christopher."

"Yes, I am, too. He had good ideas."

"I'm willing to bet this is all about financial ruin and revenge." Brother George folded his hands behind his back.

"I don't know. He was always hatching plans for our financial advancement. Far-fetched as some of them were, I'll miss his bright mind and spirit."

Brother George lowered his head and nodded. "I hope we don't lose support because of —"

"I'm sure the people who have been so generous to us in the past will continue."

Brother George smiled slightly. "You're right. I need to push my fears back."

"Trust in the Lord." Brother Morris smiled broadly.

13

Shining baby blue because of the snow, the Blue Ridge Mountains cast a benevolent presence over the rolling foothills of central Virginia. At this point the clear sky heightened the beauty of the scene. Occasional small squalls popped up, and the weatherman predicted a major storm within the week. One of the joys — or not, depending on one's temperament — of living in this blessed part of the world was the variability of the weather.

Harry thought about that as she headed east from Crozet, arriving at Jean Keelo's house in the attractive and expensive subdivision next to the Boar's Head Inn. Originally, Harry, Susan, Racquel, and Jean had planned to gather at the South River Grill, off Route 340 in Waynesboro. They could have lunch without seeing too many people they knew and therefore could stick to business. However, going over Afton Mountain, even when the roads were passable, seemed imprudent. No matter how hard crews worked, the roads iced over, given the elevation. Invariably some fool would fly by at seventy miles an hour, lose control, and spin around — if they were lucky. If not, they crashed into other cars or sailed over the guardrail to the depths below.

Harry and Susan served on the vestry board of St. Luke's. Racquel Deeds headed the refreshments committee, and Jean Keelo acted as her second banana. It had been that way since they met at Miami University. When Racquel became president of the sorority in her senior year, Jean, naturally, served as vice president.

Harry parked her truck behind Susan's Audi station wagon and Racquel's sparkling new Range Rover. She hastened to the front door, picked up the pineapple brass door knocker, and gave two sharp raps.

Jean opened the door. "Harry, come on in. Cold, isn't it?"

"Does bring a tingle to the toes," Harry agreed as she shed her coat, which Racquel hung in the small cloakroom.

Harry then handed her hostess a small, nicely wrapped Christmas present.

"Harry, you shouldn't have."

"It's a small thing, but you'll use it." Harry

had found some Crane paper with a gold pineapple on it.

Jean loved pineapples as the symbol of hospitality, plus she liked eating them.

Harry had also found some special stationery for Racquel, from the firm Dempsey & Carroll. Whereas Jean's paper was cream, Racquel's was stark white with a green grasshopper at the top. Racquel liked drinking grasshoppers. Of late, Racquel liked drinking.

Harry would give Susan her gift on Christmas Eve.

Ushered into the dining room, which was Williamsburg in inspiration, Harry hugged and kissed everyone. Women have to make a fuss or everyone assumes something is wrong. She handed Racquel her gift as she sat down. Her place was marked by a card executed with perfect penmanship and held up by a tiny brass pineapple.

"Jean, thanks for doing this, and at Christmas no less. Your tree is gorgeous."

Harry noticed that Jean had put her own card next to Harry's. As they were four and on good terms, no need for Jean to head the table. She was quite sensitive and proper about these things.

"I'll admit this to you. I hate stringing lights on a tree, and Bill makes such a fuss

". . . well" — she didn't need to mention how this could sour a holiday — "this year I hired two women to purchase a tree to my specifications and to decorate it. Victorian."

"It's stunning." Susan sipped her white wine. "Given that I have slave labor" — she meant her children, who were adults now — "I put them to work. What a mean mother I am."

They laughed because Susan, a devoted mother, had proved smart enough to know when to cut the apron strings.

Lunch started with a salad. Harry loved the tiny mandarin oranges. Next came a hot potato soup in homage to the season, and that, too, was delicious. Then Jean served the main dish, which was sliced capon with a light currant sauce, wild rice, and snow peas.

The four ate with enthusiasm. Harry, although not a gourmand — a hamburger girl, really — did appreciate that such a meal took time and thought, plus it tasted wonderful.

By the time dessert came, called "the Bomb" by Racquel, life was good. The Bomb proved to be a round ball of chocolate chip ice cream on a thin brownie with raspberry sauce drizzled over it.

"Do you call it the Bomb because it looks like a cannonball?" Susan inquired.

Racquel, on her second glass of crisp white wine, laughed. "No. The calories. It will just bomb your diet to bits."

"Honey, you don't have to worry about that," Susan complimented Racquel, who was five foot eight and rigorous about her appearance.

"You're too kind. Middle age . . ." She paused. "Let's just say when your metabolism changes you have to be vigilant."

"Oh, Racquel, you've been dieting since college," Jean, who was five foot two and tiny-boned, teased her. "Then when you had Tom and Sean you were sure you'd turn to fat. And look at you."

Racquel soaked up the praise but pretended she didn't deserve it, which she did. "We all aspire to keep trim like Harry."

"Easiest diet in the world: work on a farm," Harry said.

"How's the vineyard doing?" Jean politely asked.

"Well, you can't harvest the first year, but I had a bumper crop. Of course, without Patricia Kluge's guidance, I think I would be sending out engraved invitations to my first nervous breakdown," Harry said.

Susan added, "When Mother Nature is your partner, who knows?"

"Bryson and I visited Patricia's vineyards

at harvest time. I can't believe how much she and Bill have done." Racquel mentioned Bill Moses, Patricia's husband.

"He always says he's the only Jewish acolyte in Virginia." Harry laughed.

Patricia worshipped at a small Catholic church built on the estate. Bill always attended with her. Like many people not born to the Church of Rome, he found some solace in the ritual while sidestepping the dogma.

"This entire state is in Felicia Rogan's debt." Racquel lifted her glass to the woman who, as imposing as Juno herself, had revived the wine industry in Virginia, an occupation begun by Dr. Thomas Walker before the Revolution.

The Revolution, the War of 1812, and finally the War between the States, sixty percent of which was fought on Virginia soil, destroyed whatever progress had been made by vintners. One remarkable woman named Felicia Rogan changed all that in the 1970s, with vision, drive, and tenacity.

"I dream about a tiny vineyard but, you know, we can never leave town. Bryson needs to be close to the hospital," Racquel lamented.

"Do you ever miss it?" Susan asked.

"The hospital? Being a nurse?" Racquel's

large domed gold ring caught the light.

"Yes," Susan affirmed.

"Funny you ask that. In some ways, I do. I like the operating room. The adrenaline, the tension. It sounds crazy, but that appealed to me. You can't think of anything but what needs to be done. When you're finished, you're exhausted, but you feel you've made a small difference in the world."

Finally, they couldn't stand it anymore.

Racquel said, "Isn't it odd that we spoke of Christopher Hewitt when we made the wreaths and then . . . well, you know. What could we have done?"

Susan immediately said, "He cost some people millions with the fiasco in Phoenix."

"We may never know. Best to let the sheriff do his job," Jean replied thoughtfully.

"I suppose." Racquel hooted. "But, you know, what has occurred to me is that families are so vulnerable when one of their own is dying. Yes, the order does provide care and comfort. Bryson tells me about it. There may be Christian love involved but I think that order is becoming rich. I thought they took vows of poverty."

"Never thought of that." Harry hadn't, either.

"Like pocketing some donations?" Susan couldn't think of anything else.

"What an awful thought." Jean's hand flew to her heart.

"Cure the disease and there go the profits." Racquel's eyes narrowed. "If a disease is manageable, then profits soar."

"Do you really believe that?" Harry was aghast.

"I do. Susan, you asked if I miss nursing? What I didn't say is I don't miss the utter corruption of medicine by pharmaceutical companies and insurance companies. And let's not forget our precious government, which believes it, too, can dictate to medicine. Bryson can hardly practice anymore. It's utterly insane and so corrupt it turns my stomach. And, trust me, the vested interests protect themselves just like the oil companies. There isn't one scrap of concern for the public welfare. It's all profit-driven." She paused, somewhat surprised at her own vehemence. "When Tom was born I could retire, so to speak. If I'd stayed in medicine, I think one day I would have shot off my mouth and hurt my husband's career."

"That's dispiriting." Harry half-smiled.

Jean quietly surprised them all. "What I find dispiriting is that this entire society is sexualized. Sex is used to sell everything. We're bombarded with images, suggestions, outright taunting. Add to that the fact that we meet so many more people than our parents did or those who came before. Amidst all those people, some are bound to be, uh, delicious."

"There is that." Racquel sighed. "Which somehow makes monks strange. Then again, the Catholic Church covered up all those pedophile priests. That's as shameful as the Inquisition. Lying bastards."

"It's difficult to be compassionate when the molested were children," Harry concurred. "Sex is irrational. The impulse in one's self is irrational; the response to other people's behavior can be irrational."

"That's part of what makes monks strange," Jean said. "I grasp the significance of sacrificing your sexuality for the community. It's your gift, and if you aren't in a family then you can more easily serve others. The truth is, each of us puts our families first, and we must."

"True." Susan found herself intrigued by this discussion.

"We have thousands of years of evidence from every civilization this world has produced that no form of restraint, no punishment, can really alter the fact that people are going to have sex, whether with a socially approved partner or not." Harry believed this.

"Bryson's fooling around again," said Racquel. "I think it's time for me to have a retaliatory affair to make up for the past."

"Racquel, what does that solve?" Jean had heard this before.

"Makes me feel better. I've been married to the man for eighteen years, and, you know, it's really true that you don't know someone until you live with them. I remember on our honeymoon: we didn't exactly escalate this into an argument, but it was a pointed discussion. We stayed on the island of St. John's in the Caribbean, a wonderful place to have a honeymoon. The bathroom needed a new roll of toilet paper. Why call the maid? Especially on our honeymoon and when there were extra rolls in the bathroom. So I put the roll of paper on the holder, with the paper drawing down from the back." She paused for dramatic effect. "He comes in, I leave. He emerges and says, 'Toilet paper should always have the paper pull from the front.' I said, 'What's the difference?' It's needless to add further detail. It went on. That's when I fully realized I had married a control freak."

"Bill suffers a touch of that, too," Jean observed wryly.

"Bill's a piker compared to Bryson. I try to ignore it, but sometimes I really could kill him. And what's with Bill's homophobia? I swear he's getting worse. Even Bryson noticed."

Jean shrugged. "Middle age. He's getting cranky. Everything sets him off."

On the way home, Harry thought about the tempestuous emotions that a spouse's affair releases. She hadn't wanted to kill Fair, she just never wanted to see him again. He had a lot to learn, but so did she. Some men are players. Many aren't but succumb due to stress, a sagging sex life, or any number of reasons, all of them understandable, not that understanding means consent.

Then she thought about the toilet-paper discussion. If Fair had pulled something like that on their first honeymoon, she would have gotten up in the middle of the night and toilet-papered his car. Their honeymoon was spent in Crozet, since neither of them had money at the time.

A honeymoon is a honeymoon, and theirs, given the rupture and subsequent healing, was continuing on.

14

On the eve of the winter solstice, sun sparkling on the snow kept humans and animals happy. Since light was in short supply, the wildlife that hunted in the day hurried to find food before sunset. The birds wanted food to ward off the cold, too. For the humans, some were so out of touch with nature that they failed to realize how the shortening of the days affected them. Some were depressed. Others felt sleepy the minute the sun set. Many ate more, not realizing the cold spurred their appetites. However, the humans all knew there were four more shopping days left until Christmas.

As it was Saturday, December 20, Harry congratulated herself on getting her shopping done early. Wrapped presents, with cards attached, would be given to her friends after the St. Luke's party. Since everyone would be there — well, most everyone — she'd save gas money on deliveries. Saving money was more important to Harry than to Fair. He figured you can't take it with you, but he wasn't a spendthrift.

"What's she doing now?" Pewter rested on the windowsill of the kitchen window over the sink.

"Reading a recipe. Christmas demands special dishes. You know that," Mrs. Murphy, also on the windowsill, replied.

"Well, I wish she'd start cooking so we could get tidbits."

"Stuffed goose," Tucker dreamily said from her sheepskin bed.

"Oyster stuffing." Pewter purred.

"I don't think she uses oyster stuffing for goose." Mrs. Murphy tried to remember past Christmas meals. *"Of course, she could roast a goose and a capon. Wouldn't that be something?"*

"More for us." Pewter raised her voice.

Harry looked up from the notebook, her mother's fine handwriting still dark blue on the lined pages. "Getting pretty chatty around here."

Tucker shot out of her bed and raced to the kitchen door. *"Intruder!"*

The cats sat up to look out the window just in time to see Simon, the barn possum, scurry back through the animal hatch in the left barn door.

One minute later, Brother Sheldon, with Brother Ed in the passenger seat, rolled up in a one-ton truck.

Harry rose, saw the two monks, put on her jacket, and hurried outside. "Brother Sheldon, Brother Ed, what a welcome surprise. Please come in and have some coffee, tea, or maybe something stronger."

Brother Sheldon smiled. "Thank you, but we're here to drop off your tree. Brother Morris has us on many a mission."

The two men climbed into the back of the truck and maneuvered the symmetrical Scotch pine. Once at the edge of the tailgate, they hopped off, hoisted it, then walked it inside. Harry preceded them to open the doors. The tree was placed in a corner of the living room.

"You wrapped the bucket in red foil." Harry beamed. "That's beautiful." The two started to leave. "Let me pay you for the tree. I never did pay."

Now in the kitchen, Brother Ed said, "No. It's the brotherhood's gift to you."

Harry reached into her pocket, pulled out bills, and pressed ten dollars into each man's hand. "Please take this."

"We don't want anything," Brother Sheldon protested.

"I know you don't, but it's cold, you've

made a special trip, and, really, you've made my day." She walked over to the liquor cabinet, which was an old pie safe, and retrieved a brand-new bottle of Johnnie Walker Black. She handed it to them. "Wards off the chill."

"Yes, it does." Brother Ed liked a nip now and then.

As Harry opened the kitchen door for them to leave, she noted, "You sure have a truck full of trees. You will be making the rounds all day."

"Maybe even the night, with the traffic." Brother Sheldon frowned. "Too much buying useless stuff." He threw up his hands. "The bills aren't paid off until April and half the stuff that people received is in the trash. We need to go back to the real Christmas."

"I agree with you there. A present or two might be nice, but these days it's a glut. Even people without much money way overspend."

Brother Ed, who had a trimmed Vandyke, pulled out his gloves and said, "The American way. That's one reason I joined the brotherhood. Kind of like stop the 'merry-go-wrong' I want to get off."

"I understand," replied Harry, who did.

No sooner did the laden truck leave than Cooper pulled up. The tracks were already glossing with ice.

Tucker barked again, and Harry, seeing Cooper's well-worn Accord, put up the coffee. Harry didn't drink coffee but enjoyed making it for others.

Cooper knocked, then came in. She took off her coat, stamping the snow off her boots. "We're making up for the last few years of little snow."

"Coffee will be ready in, umm, two minutes."

"Good." Cooper carried two medium-size presents with big shiny bows. "Don't open until Christmas."

"Promise. Hold on a minute." Harry walked back to the bedroom and came out with a long, oddly shaped wrapped present. "Same applies, although once you pick it up you may know what it is." She leaned it against the wall by the kitchen door. It was a power washer, a useful present for a country person.

"Hey, a tree!"

"Brothers Sheldon and Ed just dropped it off."

Cooper put presents under the tree, which caused Pewter to investigate.

"No catnip?" The gray cat was disappointed.

"Will she tear open the wrapping?" Cooper cast a stern eye toward the living room. Pewter pointedly ignored her.

"You never know about that one." Harry poured the coffee and also put out a dish of sliced cheese and apples.

"Thank God, no cookies."

"It's a wonder all of Virginia doesn't go into sugar shock over the holidays."

They caught up. Cooper, glowing, gave an account of Lorenzo. Harry hoped this was "the one" for Cooper. They talked about Big Mim, Little Mim, the fact that Fair truly needed a partner in business. They went on to political events — always dispiriting — and finally to Brother Christopher.

"It's not a break, but it's more information." Cooper informed Harry that Christopher had received letters from an investor who felt Christopher should go back to work and pay off those who lost money.

"Contact the letter writer?"

Cooper half-smiled. "He was pissed that Christopher was dead. I suppose . . . well, I don't know. The point is, the money is lost."

"Somehow I think time lost is worse than money lost," Harry thought out loud.

"Could be." She put a piece of cheese on an apple slice, biting into it. "Any thoughts?"

"Ha. I can't believe you're asking me."

"You can get in the middle of things and you're often right, but, Harry" — Cooper

shook her head — "you take some dumb chances."

"I know," Harry admitted. "Actually, I have thought of a few things. I believe that Christopher knew his killer."

"Why?"

Tucker and Mrs. Murphy perked up to listen.

"No sign of him running away. No sign of struggle. If he'd fought, the snow would have been kicked up. No torn clothes, no bruises. Nothing knocked over."

Cooper told her, "Right."

"Another thing: if he'd run through the cut trees and the ones already in pots, he might have knocked some over. I believe he knew who killed him and didn't fear harm from whoever did it. The killer brought him down. Fast."

"It seems he didn't fear whoever cut his throat. I wonder how they could have walked behind him, though. Most of us are uncomfortable with someone directly behind us."

Harry spoke slowly. "It's a Christmas tree farm. Any ruse might work. For instance, the killer is there to buy a tree but wants Christopher to measure its height. If he stood behind him measuring, it wouldn't be so strange."

"It sure makes you wonder if you ever really know anyone." Cooper sighed.

"It's hard enough to know yourself." Harry smiled.

15

Lush dark-green pine garlands were wrapped around stairwells and adorned the top of the hand-blown twelve-pane windows. At either end of the great hall at St. Luke's, a magnificent magnolia grand flora wreath greeted celebrants as they opened three main doors to stand inside the vestibule with its coatroom, which was also decorated.

Alicia Palmer and BoomBoom Craycroft had knocked themselves out as heads of the decorating committee. They were decorated, as well. Alicia wore a shimmering dress of Christmas red, while BoomBoom wore a long white dress with expensive green bugle beadwork on the shoulders and arms. Stunning as they were separately, they were unbelievable standing side by side.

The Reverend Herbert Jones beamed at the lovely decorations and the crowd of people clearly enjoying themselves. He looked at Alicia and BoomBoom with gratitude for their work. When Alicia and BoomBoom had first announced their love, some church members pitched a fit. Most thought about it, questioned themselves in their hearts, and accepted it. That's what Herb had hoped for. What good is a Christian who doesn't think, change, and depend on compassion from one's sisters and brothers?

Resistance flowed from Bill Keelo. He had even left the church for half a year, but his wife and children missed their friends, the wonderful programs, and, most of all, they missed Herb, who practiced what he preached.

While Bill was civil to the two ladies, no one could accuse him of being accepting. A few others remained implacable, as well. They also opposed women as ministers. Dr. Bryson Deeds was an interesting case. Love between women made perfect sense to him. Love between men did not, and he voiced this one too many times. After all, some of his patients were gay men, and he visited the AIDS patients, too. On a one-to-one basis, he was a caring and fine doctor, but he assiduously avoided gay men as a group. His friendship with Bill Keelo seemed to be reinforced by their mutual dislike.

Bryson liked Brother Morris but was appalled by the brother's time of disgrace. Racquel just laughed when Bryson had wondered how any man could carry on the way Brother Morris once had. And who would sleep with such a fatty?

St. Luke's reflected Herb's outlook. Big Mim with her millions was as welcome as old Hank Malone, poor as a church mouse — not that Cazenovia, Elocution, and Lucy Fur would countenance mice in their domain. Rich, poor, intelligent, not so intelligent, old, young, all nationalities, all manner of pairings: Herb threw open the church doors for all.

His philosophy was that St. Luke's was a workshop for sinners, not a haven for saints. And Herb believed in saints, those people who suffered for others or who quietly helped throughout their lives to no fanfare.

Not that people didn't already know, but tonight demonstrated that his embrace of all drew many to him and ultimately to one another.

The fireplaces blazed at each end of the hall, which was jammed with three hundred people, give or take a few. An ebony Steinway built in 1928 was positioned between the windows in the middle. The rich tone of the big grand, rebuilt in 1989, thrilled people who loved music. This was all the accompaniment that Brother Morris, selected brothers, and the St. Luke's choir needed.

After an hour of socializing, the program began, with rousing carols interspersed with special hymns like "O Come, O Come, Emmanuel."

When Miranda Hogendobber stepped up to the dais with Brother Morris, the place fell silent with expectation. Although untrained, Miranda possessed a remarkable instrument that could melt a heart of stone. Her voice blended perfectly with the famous tenor's as they sang duets.

The magical effect added even more to a glorious night. When the program was over, the applause rolled on. The two returned for an encore, performing "O Come All Ye Faithful" first in English and then "Adeste Fideles" in Latin.

Susan Tucker, favoring her right foot, which she'd twisted slightly slipping on ice, came up next to Harry and whispered, "Best Christmas party yet."

Harry nodded through another encore.

The two singers bowed, then left the dais.

Harry and Susan made their way through the crowd to congratulate Miranda.

"Thank you." The older woman beamed. "What an honor to sing with him." She leaned forward to whisper, "I was worried that he'd be imperious, but he wasn't."

"Who could be imperious with you?" Susan complimented her.

"I put your present in the Falcon." Harry loved that Miranda drove the old Ford from the '60s, just as she drove her old truck.

"Now, you didn't have to do that." Miranda saw Aunt Tally heading for the bar and being intercepted by Big Mim. "Oh, dear, we're about to have a contretemps."

Harry and Susan looked in the direction that Miranda was looking.

"Well, the old girl has a right to her martinis." Harry laughed. "Probably why she's lived so long."

"Right. She's pickled," Susan remarked.

Miranda laughed. "Pickled or not, Aunt Tally is a handful."

Resisting her niece, whose hand gripped her elbow, Aunt Tally burst into a smile as Bill Keelo walked toward her. "Bill, to my rescue."

"Beg pardon." He pushed his black-rimmed spectacles back up the bridge of his nose.

Under her breath, Aunt Tally hissed, "Unhand me, Mimsy, or I'll crack you over the head with my cane, and I mean it."

"You've had enough," Big Mim whispered back.

"I'll be the judge of that." As Bill offered

her his arm, Aunt Tally purred, "Wasn't that the most beautiful singing?"

Big Mim conceded defeat — rare for her — turned on her heel, and bumped into Brother Speed. "I'm sorry."

The wiry fellow replied, "I've had worse bumps than that."

"Haven't we all," Big Mim agreed. "Do you ride anymore?"

"Funny you should mention that, because I was thinking about getting a job riding young horses. As long as I give back fifty percent to the brotherhood, I can work outside. It's all I know, and I'm not much good at the jobs Brother George finds for me."

"Come by the barn. Paul could use a part-time rider."

"Thank you." Brother Speed felt elated. "That is a Christmas present."

Quite a few horse people would be at the Corbett Realty Christmas party at Keswick Club. Brother Speed planned to go there after this party to see if he could find more part-time work. In fact, quite a few people would be braving the roads to go to the eastern side of the county. The Corbett party could get quite frolicsome.

Bill waited patiently at the bar while Aunt Tally stood to the side. Brother Ed jostled him, not intentionally.

"Back off, Ed."

"Sorry. I was shoved from behind," Brother Ed mildly replied.

"Right." Bill's voice dripped with sarcasm, which Brother Ed ignored.

As Bill left to hand Aunt Tally her drink, Fair, also waiting, said to Brother Ed, "Bill's been touchy lately."

"Prima donna." Brother Ed shrugged. "He's always accusing Bryson of being a prima donna, but I say it takes one to know one."

"Guess so," Fair genially replied. "The prima donnas in my life are the cats."

"Not Harry?" Brother Ed's eyebrows raised.

"No."

Brother Morris, surrounded by fans, was attempting to make his way to the bar.

With a straight face, Brother Ed said, "Here he comes with his disciples. Next performance he'll walk on water."

Fair laughed. "We'd pay to see that."

"I'll tell Brother Morris. He's very eager to fill the coffers." Brother Ed smiled.

Fair returned to Harry and Susan, handing both ladies their drinks.

"Where's yours, honey?" Harry inquired.

"I'm good." He'd had one hefty scotch on the rocks, and that was enough. "I checked.

The tonic water is Schweppes."

"Aren't you the best?" Harry squeezed his hand, then stared at Susan's drink. "When did you start drinking daiquiris?"

"Tonight. Ned's politicking, and I thought I'd live large." She laughed.

Her husband, Ned, was a first-term state representative, which was an exciting position, even if sometimes frustrating.

"Bill Keelo surprised me up at the bar," said Fair. "He was curt, borderline rude, with Brother Ed. I've never seen Bill like that."

"That's because Brother Ed used to be gay." Harry shrugged. "Bill works on my mood with this. I don't know what's happened to him, but I don't remember him being this homophobic." She turned to Susan. "What do you think?"

She dismissed it. "Oh, he's going through male menopause. The old midlife crisis. He's been irritable to everyone."

Fair waved at a client across the room. "Maybe something's come up in the family."

"Who knows?" Harry's attention was on Brother Speed, who was talking to Paul de Silva.

Then Brother Speed joined them, excitedly telling them about his hopes to work part-time at Big Mim's.

"Ever met a horse you couldn't ride?" Harry wondered.

"One or two," Brother Speed admitted.

On the way home after the party, Harry mentioned that if Brother Speed could help her with the yearlings for a month or two, it would be good. "I didn't want to open my mouth without asking you."

"Great idea. We ought to be able to afford him." Fair smiled, since he knew Brother Speed wouldn't charge much.

"Great. I'll call him tomorrow."

Tomorrow would be too late.

16

December 22 dawned overcast and cold, with gusty winds. Harry consoled herself with the idea that once on the other side of the winter solstice she'd gain about a minute of sunlight a day. She'd been up at five-thirty, and now, at seven, she'd broken the ice on all the outside water troughs and turned out the horses. In summer this routine was reversed. The horses would be in the barn now, fans cooling them, and turned out at night.

She picked stalls and threw some cookies up for Simon, the possum who lived in the hayloft along with a great horned owl and a huge blacksnake. Matilda, the snake, hibernated in the back hay bales and could give one a start, but between her, the owl, and the cats, the rodent population remained satisfyingly low.

On the other side of the county, Tony Gammell, huntsman for Keswick Hunt, performed his morning chores. The kennels sat across a paved road from the Keswick Club, which was a beautiful and exclusive haven for golfers, tennis players, and anyone who wanted to sit on the veranda to enjoy the setting. Not that anyone would be sitting out today. Last night, the same night as the St. Luke's party, the club had hosted Corbett Realty's Christmas party. Some people, either due to business or being indefatigably social, attended both parties.

When Tony walked out of the kennels after feeding the hounds, he thought to check the fence lines. No matter what he or anyone else dealing with hounds did, sooner or later one of the dogs would try to dig out. He didn't notice it at first, being intent on his fences, but on the way back he saw a lone figure on the tennis court, sitting against the chain-link fence. Anyone driving into the club by the main entrance wouldn't notice. Tony stopped. Knowing that Nancy Holt, the tennis pro, wouldn't be out in the cold, and no one else would even attempt to play in this wind, he sprinted across the lightly traveled road to the fence. As he was on the outside, he knelt down and then grasped the fence as he nearly fell over from the shock. Brother Speed, legs spread out, back against the fence, appeared to be dead. Blood covered the clay court where the body sat.

Tony rose, shaking, and ran to the other side of the court. He opened the door and hurried to the body. An intelligent man and a quick thinker, Tony knew not to touch the body. Upset as he was by the sight, he looked carefully. Brother Speed had frozen, so he'd been there for hours. His throat was slit. Taking a deep breath, Tony ran to the main office of Keswick Club, a separate entity from the hunt club. No one was at work yet, as it was only seven-fifteen. He ran back to the kennel, a bit more than a quarter mile, and grabbed his cell, which he'd perched on a ledge. He dialed 911, gave accurate information, and was told to wait where he was. He then dialed his wife, Whitney. Tony didn't realize how shaken he was until he heard his wife's voice. She, in turn, was so upset she told him to stay where he was, she'd be right there.

Within fifteen minutes Deputy Cooper drove onto the grounds of Keswick Club. She'd pulled early duty this Monday, which was fine with her. Not ten minutes later the sheriff showed up, as well.

Cooper, thin rubber gloves on her hands, already knelt in front of the handsome jockey's body. The wound, one tidy, deep cut, looked like Christopher Hewitt's wound. Photographs had to be taken and then the ambulance squad could take him away. As he was frozen stiff, he'd be sitting in the back. The thought of the corpse sitting or lying on his side in a sitting position struck Cooper as macabre.

Rick joined her. "Looks like the same M.O."

"Yes." She stood up, peeled off the gloves, and stashed them in her heavy jacket. She quickly retrieved her heavy gloves, as her fingers already were throbbing from the cold.

Rick carefully observed the corpse. "Doubt he was killed right here. No blood splattered about."

"Boss, we've got someone killing monks." Cooper put her gloved hands in her armpits.

"Two men, relatively young, from the same order." His nose felt cold so he rubbed it. "Coop, this case is beginning to really worry me."

"Yeah, me, too."

"All right. Let's go to the dogs." Rick said "dogs" instead of "hounds."

She nodded and hopped in his squad car. They drove out of the tennis-court area, turned left, and within a minute had parked behind the old Keswick Hunt Club wooden clubhouse. They walked into the kennels, where the hounds notified Tony and Whitney that two strangers had entered.

"All right, lads," Tony called to the dog hounds, the proper designation for a male foxhound. "That's enough."

Cooper flipped open her notebook as Rick asked Tony to tell him what he saw.

When Tony finished, Rick asked, "Did you know Brother Speed?"

The tall, thin man responded, "Yes. He'd come to our point-to-point races and also the steeplechase races at Montpelier. People told me he was once a jockey, a good jockey, made a lot of money — and I guess lost a lot, too." Tony thought a moment. "I liked him."

Whitney added, "He was a good hand with a horse. He always wanted to be helpful."

"Did you ever hear why he retired from being a jockey?" Cooper asked. "Other than losing money?"

"People talk," Tony replied noncommittally.

Whitney added, "We didn't believe it."

"Tell me what you heard," Rick pressed.

"That he threw a race for big money. The Arkansas Derby." When Rick and Cooper looked blank, Tony added, "It's one of the important races leading up to the Kentucky Derby."

"Follow the horses, do you?" Rick inhaled the odor of clean hounds, heard their claws click and clack as they walked on the concrete.

"Not really. Know a bit more about 'chasers. I just know the basic big races here because some of the hunt-club members have horses on the track, down at Colonial Downs, mostly."

"Did he seem to you to be a dishonest man?" Cooper kept scribbling.

A surprised look crossed Whitney's pretty features. "No. No. In fact, he would tell us sometimes — not preaching, just kind of like conversation — that we should pray, trust in the Lord. Guess he was pretty messed up on drugs back in his racing days. That will screw up anybody's judgment." She grimaced slightly. "Excuse my language."

Rick laughed. "We hear worse. In fact, we say worse." He turned to Tony. "Did you see any car lights late last night?"

"Big party across the street. We're far enough away so we didn't hear too much, but we could see cars drive in and out. We fell asleep — well, I fell asleep — at one." She looked at her husband. "He was already dead to the world. Maybe I shouldn't have said that. Anyway, I could see cars still leaving at one."

"Odd place to put a body," Tony commented.

"Convenient if the killer and the victim were at the party," Cooper said.

"You've been very helpful. If we think of anything else, we'll call." Rick shook Tony's hand, then Whitney's.

Tony asked, "Officer Cooper, is Harry going to hunt the Saddlebred that movie star — I forget her name — gave her?"

"Shortro." Cooper knew all Harry's horses but had resisted riding any of them, as she was afraid. "She says he'll be ready to go next season. Says he's really smart."

They drove to the tennis courts, then sat in the car. The heater provided comfort, since the wind would tear one to pieces.

Cooper unzipped her heavy jacket. "I'll start calling the people who were at St. Luke's to see who came to this party."

"Call Doris. She'll have a list. Save yourself time and trouble." He named the executive secretary to the head of the real estate company, Alex Corbett.

"I'm on it."

Rick hit the button to push his seat back farther and stretched out his legs. "I've searched for a connection to Christmas. The holidays are emotional land mines," he said in a flat tone of voice. "Nothing that I can find."

"Doesn't seem to be, unless this ruins

Christmas for people we don't know about. Obviously, it's ruined for the order."

Rick watched the rescue squad remove the body. "They've put their hands under his legs. Good move. Better balance than tipping him back with his legs out, bent. If his eyes weren't glassy, he'd almost look alive." He blinked, then turned to Cooper. "There has to be a connection between Christopher and Speed, apart from being Brothers of Love."

"Well, they're both dead."

"Very funny."

"Actually, there is a connection: money troubles before they became monks."

"Then let's find out how many brothers also came up short." Rick wasn't hopeful about this line of reasoning, but it might lead to something bigger.

Four hours later, Brother Speed had thawed on the stainless-steel table. Dr. Emmanuel Gibson carefully removed the brother's clothes, with the help of a young intern, Mandy Sweetwater. Removing them proved difficult because of the blood. Fabrics stuck together.

When the corpse was finally unclothed, Dr. Gibson began his careful inspection before making the first cut.

Mandy, on the other side of the corpse, said, "Eyes aren't bloodshot."

"Good." Emmanuel smiled. "So you know he wasn't choked to death."

The old doctor enjoyed working with young doctors.

As he went down the body, he talked, asking Mandy questions.

Two hours later, out of his scrubs, he called Rick.

"Dr. Gibson, what have you got for me?"

"Well, Sheriff, same cut as on Christopher Hewitt, left to right, killer behind the victim. No bruises. No sign of struggle. The killer stood behind Speed." He took a breath. "Obol under the tongue."

17

More snowflakes twirled down as Harry mucked stalls. Outside, the horses played in the snow, kicking it up and running about.

The cats cuddled on saddle blankets in the tack room, but Tucker stuck with Mom. The corgi dashed out of a stall.

Harry leaned the large pitchfork against the stall and walked into the center aisle.

Tucker barked, *"Cooper!"*

Pewter opened one eye. *"Can't that dog shut up?"*

Opening the large double doors, Harry waved for Cooper to come inside the stable.

Stamping her feet, Cooper walked in.

"Coffee?"

"This time it's my turn for hot cocoa," Cooper said.

"Sounds like a winner to me." Harry smiled as she led Cooper into the cozy room, redolent of sweet feed and leather with a hint of Absorbine, used to soothe aching muscles.

"Harry." Cooper sank into one of the director's chairs. "Brother Speed was found dead this morning. Same M.O. as Christopher."

"Oh, no." Harry put the cocoa tin down lest she drop it.

Both cats opened their eyes wide now, and Tucker sat beside Cooper.

"Tony Gammell found him on the tennis courts at the Keswick Club."

"Good Lord. I hope Nancy wasn't at work."

"Luckily, Nancy Holt didn't have any tennis lessons because of the high winds and snow."

"Well, she's tough enough to go out in anything. I bet this upset Tony, too."

"Did."

Harry sat down, waiting for the water to boil. "I don't get it."

"I don't, either. You knew Brother Speed."

"Sure. He was a good horseman as well as rider."

"What do you mean?"

"Oh, there are plenty of people who can ride a horse, but a horseman is someone who truly knows how to care for horses as well as how to train them. Not a whole lot of those, and Speed was good. Very sensitive." Harry appreciated that quality.

"Ever see him gamble?"

"No."

"What about Christopher?"

"He ran football pools — pretty primitive, but it was high school."

"Ever see or hear about either one getting in trouble with women, especially married women?"

"Christopher left Crozet to go to college, so I didn't hear anything. Who knows? As for Brother Speed, well, a racing life is full of temptation."

"Both gambling and sex can run away with people, like drugs and alcohol. I'm looking for any kind of motivation for murder. Welched debts or angry spouses could qualify. Sometimes old habits reappear."

Harry thought about that. "I suppose it is hard to break an addiction, whatever it may be. But don't you think the other brothers would know or at least suspect that Speed and Christopher were struggling?"

"Time for another visit to the monastery." Cooper rubbed her eyes. "I'm tired."

"Low-pressure system. Running into walls will poop you out, too."

"I've been doing enough of that," Cooper ruefully said.

"Maybe the murderer was abused by a priest or a monk. Given the breadth of the abuse in America, it's not a long jump to assume that there are some people in Albemarle County who were molested. Maybe not by local priests but elsewhere." She added, "There are so many new people to the area, and we don't know their histories. The old families you know for generations. I mean, look at the Urquharts." She mentioned Big Mim's maiden name. "Someone could have just lost it. Maybe the abuse started one Christmas. Who knows?"

"Once the trigger of an old, buried emotion is pulled, you can't unpull it." Cooper considered Harry's idea.

"The thing about the Brothers of Love is they'd be easy to get to. They're out with the public, at the hospice, at the tree farm. If only we could figure out the reason . . . at least it would lead to potential culprits."

Cooper rose and walked to the hot plate. "Water's boiling."

"I'm not being a good hostess."

"Hey, I'm your neighbor. You don't have to dance attendance on me."

Harry smiled. "Haven't heard that phrase since my grandmother."

"That's what mine said. I think that generation used language better than we do. Their speech was so colorful. Now people imitate whatever they hear on TV or pick up off the

Internet. Pretty boring." Cooper poured water into her hot-chocolate powder, then poured water over Harry's cocoa.

She returned to the director's chair, which faced an old tack trunk serving as a coffee table.

"How nice to be waited on in my own tack room. Every time I go to Big Mim's barn or Alicia's, I suffer a fit of envy. My God, those tack rooms could be in *Architectural Digest.*" She looked around. "But this is tidy and it's mine."

"That's what counts." Cooper settled in, grateful for the hot chocolate. "Let's go over what we do know."

"Sure."

"Not much," Pewter sassed.

"Two men, late thirties, early forties. In fact, Brother Speed turned forty on December eleventh. Both of them belonged to the same order. Both raised Catholics. Both nice-looking men. Christopher was divorced. Speed never married."

Harry jumped in. "Both ruined by money troubles."

"Yep." Coop's notebook was filled with notes from questioning people. "Women just loved Speed. Probably because they could pick him up and throw him around."

"Ha." Harry appreciated that. "Wouldn't

that be fun? I can barely get Fair's feet off the ground, and he even helps by standing on his tiptoes. He can bench-press me with one hand."

"He is one big, strong man. Good thing, too. His patients outweigh him by about a thousand pounds." Cooper returned to the murders. "Both men had good personalities. People liked them. The calls I made to Phoenix — despite what Christopher did, people mentioned over and over again how likable he was. Can you think of anything I missed?"

"Both were estranged from their families."

"Right. Forgot that. They were likable but not to their folks."

"I expect they were still likable to them, but when you go through alcoholism and drug abuse with someone, I think a lot of times the family gets burned out. Plus, they don't believe anything the addict tells them. Too many lies. Christopher's family couldn't handle the scandal," Harry added.

"Anything else?"

"Their manner of death appears to be the same. Killed from behind. I take it there was no sign of struggle with Speed?"

"We'll know more after the autopsy, but no apparent sign of struggle."

"And I assume Brother Speed was killed

quickly, too. You'd think someone would have missed him up at the monastery."

"Rick called. Brother George said they figured he'd stayed overnight in town, given the roads and the fact that the party rolled on. George was scared." She paused. "You know, when we catch the killer, I wouldn't be surprised if he gets off somehow."

Harry nodded. "Everything's backward. We punish the victim. We give money to people who won't work. Old men sit in the legislature and send young men and women to their deaths. It's all backward."

"You and I aren't going to fix it."

"I think we can, but it's going to take more than just us. Like these murders. We can't bring back the dead, but if we use our wits and have a bit of luck, we'll get him."

"Think it's only one person?"

"I don't know. You'd know better than I do."

"I'm not sure. If only I could figure out the Brothers of Love connection."

"Doesn't seem to be coincidence." She frowned. "We don't know what we don't know."

"Yep." Cooper drained her hot chocolate. "Mind if I make another?"

"Course not."

"Need more?"

"I'm good."

Cooper filled the teakettle. Harry always kept a couple of bottles of distilled water in the tack room for that purpose. "I've even tried to make odd connections. For instance: facial hair."

"No connection. Speed was clean shaven and Christopher had that flaming beard."

"I know." A note of irritation crept into Coop's voice. "I'm saying that I'm looking at everything. The things that are important to a killer are not immediately obvious."

"I understand that. Kind of like the serial killer who kills women who resemble his high school crush who rejected him."

"Exactly." Cooper stood over the teakettle.

"A watched pot never boils," Harry intoned the old saying.

"Right." Cooper flopped down in the director's chair.

"They were both nice-looking. So far no ugly brothers have been killed," Harry said.

"Well, that's something."

"See, I told you they don't know a thing," Pewter said smugly.

"Crabby Appleton." Mrs. Murphy used the childhood insult. *"They know a lot. Didn't you listen?"*

"She only listens to herself talk." Tucker rolled her eyes.

"I am sick and tired of being insulted by one snotty cat and one bubble butt." Pewter showed her claws for effect. *"It's someone who hates Christmas."*

Her idea was as good as anyone else's.

18

"Don't lie to me."

"Racquel, I'm not lying to you." Bryson felt exhausted.

"I know the signs."

"I'm distracted, tired, and Christmas isn't my favorite season."

Both their sons were at the ice rink in downtown Charlottesville. Without the restraining influence of her children, Racquel let her emotions get the better of her.

"Who is she?"

"I swear to you I am not having an affair with a nurse, a secretary, a nurse's aide, or any other woman."

"One of those caretakers at the hospice is pretty. I noticed when I visited Aunt Phillipa."

"I'm not." He walked to the bar to fix himself a scotch on the rocks. "I am worried about the Brothers of Love. The murders could hurt donations. No one does what they do. They're . . . well, you've seen the care."

"Have." Her eyes narrowed. "You do seem depressed. Maybe the affair is over."

"Racquel, sometimes you make it hard to love you."

"Ditto." She strode to the bar. "Martini."

He fixed her a dry one and they sat by the fire. "I've made mistakes. I was wrong. I can't say more than that. How can we go forward if you mistrust me?"

"It's hard to trust you. You're accomplished at deceit."

He took a long draft. "I'm sorry."

"Don't men ever consider the damage they do for what amounts to fifteen minutes of pleasure?"

"Obviously not. But I am not having an affair. I told you that. You are the only woman in my life."

"What would you do if I had an affair?"

"I don't know."

"It might be painful to have the shoe on the other foot."

"Yes. Look, can't we call a truce? It's Christmas. The tension is so thick in this house you can cut it. For the boys' sake."

"I'll try."

"Thought I'd go over to Alex's later for a poker game, but I'll cancel. It'd be nice to have a little time together before the kids come back."

She brightened at this and downed her martini. "Good idea."

19

The snow-covered Leyland cypress swayed hypnotically in the wind. Harry, once again up since five-thirty, surveyed the orderly plantings of Waynesboro Nurseries's stock on Tuesday morning. She'd arranged to have twelve of these lovely trees planted at Fair's office as a Christmas present. Naturally, the evergreens wouldn't go in the ground until spring, but she wanted to double-check to make certain of her decision.

Landscaping came naturally to Harry, probably because she loved it. She joked with her husband that if God gives you the skills in one department, he often leaves out another. This was by way of explaining her terrible taste in any clothing that didn't involve equine pursuits. Once every two or three years, Susan would drag her to Nordstrom's, often aided by BoomBoom, a clotheshorse.

After she'd conversed with Tim Quillen at

the nurseries, she felt that itch to get something for herself, so she called Jeffrey Howe at Mostly Maples and ordered two good old-fashioned sugar maples, also to be planted in the spring.

She cranked the motor on the 1978 Ford, but before she could leave, her cell rang. Harry didn't like to drive and talk on the phone, so she stayed put.

"Hello."

"Honey, can you swing by Southern States and pick up extra halters and lead shanks? I forgot," Fair said.

"Sure, honey." Fair always kept extras in his truck just in case.

"How's your day so far?" Harry inquired.

"Good, but it will be better when I'm home with you."

When she clicked off her cell, she had a smile on her face.

In about thirty-five minutes she was back in Charlottesville, and she dropped by Bryson Deeds's office. Harry had washed and dried Racquel's pottery dishes from St. Luke's Christmas party and offered to drop them off at the house, but Racquel told her to leave them at Bryson's office. He would still be seeing patients right up to Christmas Eve, and she was doing last-minute shopping.

No one sat at the reception desk, so Harry put the dishes on the reception counter. As she walked out into the hall of the medical office building, she heard a door close behind her.

Brother Luther strode up to her.

"Merry Christmas, Brother Luther."

His eyes darted around. "Merry Christmas to you."

Noticing how nervous he was, she thought to console him. "If you're a patient of Bryson's, you're in good hands. He's a wonderful cardiologist."

"Oh, I have a little heart murmur. Nothing to worry about. It's extra fluttery. All these terrible events."

"I'm so sorry."

He grasped her hand. "Harry, if anything happens to me, call my brother in Colorado Springs." He pulled a little notebook out of his coat pocket and scribbled the name.

Harry read it, "Peter Folsom. I didn't know your last name was Folsom." She smiled at him. "Your heart will tick along, but I promise I'll call him. But, really, Brother Luther, don't worry. You'll just make yourself sick."

He let go of her hand. "Someone out there is killing us. Our order. I could be next."

"Maybe it isn't about the order. Maybe it's

those brothers' pasts catching up with them."

He leaned down and whispered in her ear, even though no one was around. "It's the order, and the past catches up with all of us."

"Brother Luther, forgive me, but I can't imagine what Christopher — I mean, Brother Christopher — or Brother Speed did to provoke such an" — she searched for the right word — "end."

"You don't want to know." With that, he scuttled down the hall.

20

Mrs. Murphy, Pewter, and Tucker, upset that Harry did not take them along for her errands, sat in front of the living-room fireplace. Embers still glowed from last night's fire, a testimony to slow-burning hardwoods.

"Low-pressure system coming in," Pewter drowsily announced.

"Windy now." Tucker could hear the reverberations at the top of the flue as well as see the trees bending outside the windows.

"Something's behind it." Mrs. Murphy felt the change in atmospheric pressure, too.

"It's cozy right here. I wish Mom would get back, to start up the fire." Pewter snuggled farther down in the old throw on the sofa.

"She should have taken us," Mrs. Murphy grumbled. *"We can't even tear up the tree, because she hasn't decorated it. Of course, we could shred the silk lamp shades."*

Tucker advised, *"Wouldn't do that. Tomorrow is Christmas Eve. She won't give you your presents."*

"You're right," the tiger acknowledged. *"We could go for a walk."*

"There's a storm coming. Besides, why get your paws cold?" Pewter enjoyed her creature comforts.

"Well, I can't rip anything to pieces. I don't feel like sleeping just yet. I'll go visit Simon." With that, Mrs. Murphy bounced down from the sofa, walked to the kitchen, and slipped out the dog door, then through the second dog door in the screened-in porch.

"Hey, wait for me." Tucker hastened after her.

Pewter thought they were nuts.

Tucker caught up with the sleek cat just as she slipped through the dog door at the barn. Once inside, they both called up for Simon.

"Shut up down there, groundling," Flatface, the great horned owl, grumbled from the cupola. *"You two could wake the dead."*

Simon shuffled to the edge of the hayloft. *"Got any treats?"*

"No," both replied.

The gray marsupial sighed. *"Oh, well, I'm glad to see you anyway."*

"Mom will bring you treats for Christmas. You, too, Flatface. I think she has some meat pies with mince for you," Mrs. Murphy called

up to the fearless predator.

Flatface opened one eye, deciding that her afternoon nap was less important than hearing about her present. She dropped down, wings spread so she could glide, and landed right next to Simon, who was always amazed at her accuracy.

"Mom would even give Matilda a Christmas present if she weren't hibernating." Tucker laughed, for her human truly loved all animals.

Matilda, the blacksnake, grew in girth and size each year and had reached impressive proportions. In the fall she had dropped onto Pewter from a big tree in the backyard, nearly giving the fussy cat a heart attack. Both Mrs. Murphy and Tucker were careful not to bring it up, because Pewter would rant at the least, swat them at the worst.

"What's mince?" Flatface asked.

"I don't know," Tucker replied.

"It's things cut up into tiny pieces," answered Mrs. Murphy. *"Mom makes a meat pie; the meat is minced, but she adds other things to it and it's kind of sweet. I saw her baking pies, and I know she made a small one for you."*

"What's she giving me?" Simon hoped it was as good as a mince pie.

"She's making you maple syrup icicles.

She's got a bag of marshmallows, too, and I think she's made up a special mash for the horses. I saw her cooking it all, but I don't know what she's put into it. She'll warm it up Christmas morning. Maybe she'll give you some."

"Goody." His whiskers twitched.

Flatface, not always the most convivial with four-legged animals, was feeling expansive. *"I saw something strange."* When the others waited for her to continue, she puffed out her considerable chest and said, *"I was flying up along the crest of the mountains. Wanted to see what was coming in across the Shenandoah Valley. When I came back, I swooped down toward all those walnut trees in the land that Susan Tucker inherited from her uncle, the old monk."* She paused, shifted her weight, then continued. *"Well, you know there are all those old fire trails leading off both sides of the mountain's spine. I saw two men in a Jeep heading down toward the walnut stand. So I perched in a tree when they stopped. They got out and put a big green metal box next to the first set of boulder outcroppings. They opened the box — it was full of money — counted it, put the money back, and shut the box. They left it there."*

Simon stared at Flatface. Mrs. Murphy

and Tucker looked at each other, then up to the owl.

"Did you know who they were?" Tucker inquired.

"No, but a sticker with the caduceus on it was on the windshield of the Jeep." Flatface, with her fantastic vision, could pick out a mouse from high in the air. Seeing a sticker was easy.

Tucker swept her ears forward. *"That sounds like a lot of money."*

"Is," Flatface chirped low.

Mrs. Murphy, mind flying, inquired, *"Was there a lock on the box?"*

"No. It's one of those toolboxes like Harry uses. I can lift up the latch with my talon and then slip the U ring over the latch. Easy as mouse pie." She glanced down at Mrs. Murphy's paws. *"Your claws are long enough to lift up the latch. Don't know if you could pull over the U ring. Might could."*

"What did you see over the valley?" Tucker wondered.

"Snowstorm's building up. Be here in another two hours, maybe a little longer. It's big. Can't you feel it coming?"

"Sure," Simon piped up, then flattered the large bird. *"But you can fly up the mountain and see everything. You're the best weather predictor there is."*

Flatface blinked appreciatively. *"Batten down the hatches."*

Their entrance covered by a tack trunk, the mice living behind the walls tittered as the two friends left the barn.

The oldest male grumbled, *"Mouse pie."*

Once outside, Mrs. Murphy turned to Tucker and said, *"Come on. We've got enough time."*

The cat and dog, moving at a brisk trot, covered the back hundred acres in no time. The land rose gently on the other side of the deep creek. The angle grew sharper as they climbed upward. At a dogtrot, the walnut stand lay twenty-five minutes from the barn. The animals knew the place well, not only because Susan and Harry routinely checked the walnuts and other timber but because a large female bear lived in a den in one of the rock outcroppings. They knew the bear in passing, often chatting with her on the back acres or commenting on her cubs.

As they reached the walnut trees, the wind picked up a little. At the edge of the big stand — acres in itself — they saw the green metal box, which had been tucked under a low ledge just as Flatface described it.

Tucker put her paw behind it and pushed it away from the huge rock.

"I can pop it." Mrs. Murphy exposed her

claws, hooked one under the small lip, lifted up the latch, then hooked the upper U latch and pulled it over.

"I can press the release button." Tucker hit the metal square button in the middle of the latch.

The latch clicked and the lid lifted right up. Thousands of dollars, each packet bound by a light cardboard sleeve, nestled inside.

"Wow," Tucker exclaimed. *"That's a lot of Ben Franklins."*

"Why put the box here? All this money?" The tiger was intrigued but confused, as well.

"Why are there dead men's faces on money?" Tucker touched her nose to the money.

"It's supposed to be a high honor."

"Murphy, how can it be an honor if you're dead? Benjamin Franklin doesn't know his face is on a bill."

"I don't know. Humans think differently than we do." Mrs. Murphy thought it was odd, too. *"Tucker, carry one of these packets back. I'll put the lid down."*

The corgi easily lifted out the packet. Mrs. Murphy pushed the lid down, and the tongue of the latch fit right into the groove. She didn't bother to flip the U over the top of the latch.

The two hurried back down the mountainside. Every now and then Tucker would stop and drop the packet to take a deep breath. She was getting a little winded and needed to breathe from her mouth as well as her nostrils.

By the time they reached the back door, Harry's 1978 F-150 sat in the drive. They burst through the two dog doors.

"Where have you two been? I've looked all over for you."

Pewter sat beside Harry. The gray cat was as upset as Harry. Lazy as she could be, she didn't like being left out, and they had taken off without telling her.

"Busy," Mrs. Murphy replied as Tucker dropped the money.

"What have you got?" Harry reached down and picked it up, her jaw dropping as she flipped through ten thousand dollars. "What the hell!"

To hold ten thousand dollars in cash in her hand took her breath away. She sat down hard in a kitchen chair and recounted the money.

"There's more. You'll be rich!" Tucker wiggled her tailless rear end.

"Think of the tuna that will buy," Pewter purred. *"Let's go get the rest of it."*

"We can't do it without Mom," Mrs. Murphy

advised. *"The rest of it is in a metal toolbox."*

"You carried that. We should all go, and we have to hurry because a storm is coming. We could bring it here. Think of the food, the cat-nip!" Pewter displayed a rare enthusiasm.

Harry peered down at her friends. "Where'd you get this?"

"I thought you'd never ask." Tucker walked to the door, then looked over her shoulder at Harry.

Over the years, Harry had learned to pay attention to her animals. For one thing, their senses were much sharper than her own. Then, too, they had never let her down, even Pewter, who grumbled far too much. She'd followed Tucker and the cats before, so she knew the signs and, clearly, Tucker had a mission.

"All right." She rose, pulled her heavy coat off the peg, wrapped a plaid scarf around her neck, and took the cashmere-lined gloves from the pockets.

"How far is it?" Pewter inquired.

"Walnut stand," Tucker answered.

"Mmm, well, since she's got the message, I'll hold down the fort."

"Pewter, you are so lazy," Mrs. Murphy said. *"You were the one who said, 'Let's go get the rest of it.' "*

"It's cold. And there really is no reason for all

of us to go." With that, she turned and sashayed back into the living room, where Harry had restoked the fire.

"Can you believe her?" Mrs. Murphy was incredulous.

Tucker laughed. *"Right, she volunteered to carry money."*

"You're talking about me," Pewter called from the living room. *"Because I'm so fascinating."*

Harry opened the door, then the screen door, and stepped out to see a rapidly changing sky. Clouds rolled lower now, dark clouds piling up behind the Blue Ridge Mountains. Wouldn't be long before they'd slip over. She could just make out gusts of snow in some high spots. If only the dog and cat could talk, she'd take the truck. She started walking behind the two, who were already shooting ahead of her. The Thinsulate in her boots sure helped, as did the wool-and-cashmere-blend socks. Much as Harry refrained from spending money, she had sense to spend it on good equipment and warm work clothes.

The remnants of the last snow crunched underfoot. By the time they all reached the creek, she followed the two over the narrowest place, her heel just breaking the ice at the edge. She didn't get wet, though, so she smiled and picked up her pace, since the animals had started trotting.

"Sure hope we can get up and back before this hits." Mrs. Murphy sniffed the air. *"It's higher up there, so I bet the flurries are already swirling."*

"Even if it snows harder, we'll make it," Tucker replied optimistically.

"As long as we can see. A whiteout scares me." The cat felt the barometric pressure slide a bit more.

"If only she could move faster." Tucker looked back at Harry striding purposefully along.

"She can run, but with all those clothes on she can't run for long." Mrs. Murphy fluffed out her fur, for it now felt even colder.

Even with the weight of her coat and the sweater underneath, Harry could keep up, as long as the two kept it at a trot. She reached the walnut stand in a half hour, snow falling thicker now.

"Over here." Tucker bounded to the outcropping.

"Someone's coming." Mrs. Murphy heard a motor cut off perhaps a quarter of a mile away.

Tucker heard it, too. *"We'd better hurry."*

Harry reached the box protected by the low rock overhang. Just then a gust of wind sent snow flying everywhere. The denuded walnut tree bent slightly, and the pines beyond bowed as if to a queen.

She knelt down, opened the box. The crisp bills, neatly stacked, promised some ease in her life. However, Harry, raised strictly by her parents, would never take money that wasn't hers. She'd turn this over to Cooper, as she realized immediately that something was terribly wrong. This had to be blood money, more or less.

She didn't realize how wrong things were, even though Tucker barked loudly and Mrs. Murphy leapt up on the overhang. The wind, whistling now, obscured sound to human ears. Harry never saw what was coming. One swift crack over the head and she dropped.

Tucker started to attack, but Mrs. Murphy screamed, *"Leave him. He wants the money, not Mom."*

She was right. Brother George hurried back up to the old fire road before the snow engulfed him.

Tucker licked Harry's face. Mrs. Murphy jumped down. A trickle of blood oozed down the side of Harry's head. Her lad's cap had fallen off.

"I can't wake her." Tucker frantically licked.

"She's alive. I hope her skull isn't cracked." The cat sniffed Harry's temples. *"Tucker, Fair*

should be home. You have to get him. I'll stay here. This storm is only going to get worse. Help me push her cap back on. At least she won't lose so much heat from her head."

"I can't leave you all."

"Tucker, you must. She'll suffer frostbite if she's here too long. She might even freeze to death. And if she wakes, what if she's disoriented? I don't know if I can get her home. You have to go NOW."

The dog touched noses with her dearest friend, licked Harry one more time.

"I'll see you." The mighty little dog left them.

Tucker ran for all she was worth, goaded by both fear and love.

Mrs. Murphy curled around Harry's head. The low overhang offered some protection. It wasn't so bad, the tiger told herself. She desperately wanted to believe that as the world turned white.

21

"Thanks, Coop. Call me on my cell, okay?" Fair punched the off button.

He'd arrived home an hour ago. Harry's beloved truck sat in the driveway. He assumed she was in the barn. But when Tucker failed to rush out and greet him, he poked his head inside. No Harry. Not a sign of her in the house. Pewter meowed incessantly, even though Fair had no idea what the cat was telling him.

He wasn't a worrier by nature, but what set him off was ten thousand dollars in one-hundred-dollar bills, bound by a cardboard sleeve, sitting on the kitchen table, big as you please.

Where did Harry get the money? Why would she just leave it on the kitchen table? This was so out of character for his wife that he had called Cooper to find out if she was over there. Cooper's farm was the old Jones family place, which the young detective rented from Reverend Herb Jones.

Cooper, also at a loss over the money, was now worried herself.

Fair called her back. "Hey, I'm sorry to bother you again, but I just noticed the sleeve on this wad of bills has teeth marks."

"Human?" Cooper was more than intrigued.

"No. Looks like a dog or a very big cat." He looked in Pewter's direction and she pointedly turned away.

"Fair, I'll be right over."

"Coop, I don't want to trouble you."

"Too late."

Within seven minutes she rolled down the driveway. Snow was falling steadily now.

"Jesus, you burned the wind getting here." Fair laughed, trying to make light of his fear.

"Show me the money." She smiled, but she was as worried as he was.

He pointed to the kitchen table, Pewter now sitting on one chair.

"They're up at the walnut stand, and I bet you can't see the hand in front of your face up there," Pewter told them, even though she knew it was hopeless.

Cooper sat down. She didn't touch the money, just stared at the sleeve. "Teeth marks, all right." She looked up at the tall vet. "Maybe she dropped the money and

Tucker picked it up."

"That's as good an explanation as any, but we both know Harry wouldn't just put money like this on the table, and if she took it out of her bank account, she'd tell me."

"Not if it's your Christmas present."

"Cash?" He was surprised.

"Maybe she's buying something big."

"With cash?" He inhaled sharply. "Do you know something I don't?"

"Yeah, about a lot of things, but not about your Christmas present."

He appreciated her humor, which took off the edge. "Right."

"I take it you keep separate bank accounts?"

"We do, but we have a joint account to cover the farm costs." He sat down opposite Cooper, who now turned the money over in her hands. "Something's wrong."

"Maybe." She thought so, too.

"Should we call Rick?"

"Not without a body." The minute the words fell out of her mouth, Cooper repented. "I don't mean that."

"I know. Unfortunately, there have been bodies."

"Harry's not a monk. If she is, it's news to me."

"Given that we found Christopher, she

can't help but stick her nose in it; that's her nature. Much as I love her, I could smack her upside the head right now. What if she's run up on the killer?"

Cooper studied the money for too long, then her eyes met Fair's. "I know. I guess I haven't done the job of a friend, which is to calm and console you."

He smiled wanly. "I don't want consolation. I want my wife."

Barking made them both sit up. Pewter ran to the dog door just as Tucker burst through it.

"Hurry! Hurry!" The corgi turned in tight circles, pushed though the door, then leapt back in again, only to repeat the process.

Fair threw his coat on, with Cooper right behind him. Pewter brought up the rear.

"What's wrong?" the gray cat asked the dog, who was tired but ready to go all the way back up again.

"Brother George hit her over the head and took the money. She didn't see him, and we didn't, either, until the last minute. High winds, could hardly hear. Blew scent away, and sometimes you couldn't see." The dog caught her breath. *"Heard the motor cut off way up on the fire road. That was it."*

"Is Harry all right?"

"I don't know. She was unconscious when I

left, and Murphy is with her."

Pewter, now running with the corgi, said nothing. Insouciant as she might appear, at bottom she loved her little family, and if that meant going out in what was becoming a whopper of a storm, then she was going.

Tucker, realizing the humans couldn't keep up, slowed. She'd forgotten for a moment about the fact that they followed on two feet, encumbered by winter wear.

She barked loudly.

Fair responded, "Hold hard, Tucker."

Pewter, waited, closed her eyes. The snow, coming hard in swirling winds, stung her eyes.

"I'm glad you're with me," Tucker panted.

"It's my new exercise program." Pewter saw Fair's huge frame loom in the snow, Cooper's smaller one beside him.

Tucker knew how worried Pewter was. For one thing, she would never admit she was fat — and she just did. The dog turned to face the onslaught, Pewter shoulder to shoulder with her.

The humans kept up, since Tucker trotted now. Fortunately, the snow wasn't deep yet. Footing could be dicey in those places where the old snow had hardened like vanilla icing, and in some spots, there was nothing but ice.

They pressed on, balloons of steam coming from four mouths, four heads down against the wind, which sounded like a Mercedes at full throttle.

As they began to climb, conditions worsened, but the exhausted dog never faltered, nor did the gray cat. Behind them, the humans — who were wiping the snow from eyes and eyelashes, breath coming sharper now — knew they had to keep going and stay together.

Slowed by conditions, they reached the walnut stand in forty minutes instead of thirty.

Tucker called, *"Murphy!"*

"Here!"

Even with the wind, the two humans heard the piercing meow.

Pewter raced to her friend, Tucker alongside, with Fair and Cooper almost at their heels, rejuvenated by Mrs. Murphy's voice.

They found the cat draped over Harry's head, her tail swishing to keep the snow from pasting Harry's eyes and filling up her nostrils.

Fair and Cooper knelt down, and Cooper gently lifted the cap.

"God damn, that's nasty," she cursed.

Fair took Harry's pulse, fingers cold since he'd pulled off his glove. "Strong."

The snow had already covered the blood as

well as Brother George's tracks.

"Maybe we can rig up a sled like the Indians used: two poles crossed. I'll put my coat on them to hold her," Cooper offered.

"No tools. I can carry her down, but it will take a while."

"I can do the fireman's carry. Spell you."

"You're a good woman, Coop. Remind me to tell you that more often."

Tucker and Pewter huddled around Mrs. Murphy, who was half frozen herself.

"Can you make it?" Tucker asked.

"Yeah." Mrs. Murphy stretched, then shivered.

Fair touched the cat's snow-covered head. "God bless you, Mrs. Murphy." He looked over to Cooper. "You could carry her for a bit."

"Will do."

Fair stood back up, shook his legs, then knelt down and lifted Harry. Since he was accustomed to patients that weighed 1,200 pounds, Fair's five-foot-seven-inch, one-hundred-forty-two pound wife felt light enough. He knew as time wore on she'd feel heavier and heavier, though.

He used the fireman's carry and they began the trek down, at times hardly able to see. The ruts in the old wagon trail began to fill up, pure white with no rocks protruding. A few saplings here and there helped keep their bearings. Tucker and Pewter, better able to keep on track, also helped. Tucker barked if anything needed to be sidestepped or if the humans began to lose their way.

After twenty minutes, slipping and sliding now, Fair gently laid down Harry. He bent over, hands on knees, and gulped in air.

"I'll take a turn." Cooper was taller than Harry and accustomed to lifting human burdens on occasion — since a cop's duties require many strange moments with truly strange people. The deputy grunted, but she hoisted Harry on her shoulders and stood up. "I won't last as long as you did."

"A breather helps." He scooped up Mrs. Murphy, opening his coat and putting her inside, then zipping it back up, with her head outside for air.

To her surprise, Cooper lasted fifteen minutes, almost the rest of the way down the mountain.

She and Fair exchanged burdens. Mrs. Murphy noted that Pewter, quick to want to be carried, made not one peep.

Tucker and Pewter, wind to their tails now, pushed ahead. Occasionally the wind would swirl, a white devil blowing snow into their eyes and mouths again, but they turned their heads sideways, keeping on, always keeping on.

When they reached the creek, Fair again took a breather, sweat pouring over his forehead, little icicles forming.

Cooper picked up Harry again and struggled through the creek, as there was no way to jump it. Some water crept into her boots where the soles had worn. The shock of the frigid water energized her for a little bit, although her legs had begun to weaken. Her back was holding up, but her quads burned. She knew she couldn't make it too long, and she hoped she could get back to the farm on her own steam.

Ten minutes seemed like a lifetime. Cooper faltered, lurched, and slowly sank to her knees so as not to drop Harry.

"You okay?" Fair knelt beside her.

She nodded, gasping for breath. "You hear stories," she gulped again, "about guys carrying wounded buddies for miles in wartime." Gulped again. "Heroes."

In a quiet voice he said, "Love comes in many forms. Sometimes I think it's disguised as duty. Are you sure you can make it?"

"I'm sure. Get her back. I'll get there."

"I'm not leaving you. This will turn into a real whiteout. You could be one hundred yards from the barn and not know it. We've got to stick together or we might not make it."

"Okay. Let me see if my cell will work now." She knew she usually couldn't get a signal on the mountainside.

Fair handed Mrs. Murphy to Cooper, who put her in her coat, and Fair hoisted up Harry again.

Finally Cooper got a signal and called an ambulance. The line crackled, but she could hear and so could they. She told them to come to the Haristeens'. Next she called Rick.

Twenty minutes later, after Fair and Cooper took more breaks, they finally stumbled through the back door.

The ambulance arrived a few minutes after they did. Fair hadn't even taken his coat off before the attendants bounded the gurney into the living room, where he and Cooper had placed Harry on the sofa.

"I'll go with her," Fair said.

"I'll follow you with the truck," replied Cooper.

"Don't do that. You've done enough."

"Won't be long before the roads are treacherous and the only thing out there will be emergency vehicles. Also, I have my badge just in case. With any luck you can bring her home."

Too tired to argue, he gratefully acceded. "I'll see you there."

Given the weather and the wrecks on the road, they made it to the emergency room in fifty minutes. Normally the trip would take thirty minutes.

Rick met Cooper there.

Back at the house, a warming Mrs. Murphy licked her paws. *"Thanks, Pewter."*

"Don't think I'll do it again." Pewter was feeling sufficiently relieved to sass.

Tucker and Murphy looked at each other, then the tiger cat rubbed across the dog's broad chest, thanking her.

"Let's pray that Mom is okay," Tucker said.

"Take more than a crack on the head to keep her down," Mrs. Murphy said, and the other two hoped she was right.

22

Since it was December 23, the staff at the hospital functioned at skeleton level. Fortunately, Dr. Everett Finch, a friend of Fair's, was on duty in the ER. He X-rayed Harry's skull and, to be safe, ran an MRI.

Fair, worn out, slumped on a bench in the corridor, Cooper beside him. She'd fallen asleep from the tremendous effort of getting Harry down from the walnut stand.

The doors swung open and Everett walked up to them. "She's fine. No cracked skull. A concussion, sure enough, but she'll be okay."

Tears welled up in Fair's blue eyes. "Thank God."

Cooper, awake now, also misted up.

"She's coming to. She may be nauseated, throw up. And there is some chance her vision will be blurred. You never really know with these things. And I can just about guarantee you that she will remember nothing, maybe not even the pain of being clobbered." He paused. "Any idea who did this?"

"No," Fair answered. "We don't know why she walked halfway up the mountain with a storm coming. She can read the weather better than the weatherman, so you know whatever happened up there, it was important. I hope she can tell us something."

"I suggest we keep her overnight and you pick her up in the morning."

Alert now, Cooper asked, "You're at barebones staff, right?"

"Holidays." Everett smiled.

"Fair, we can't leave her here. We know whoever attacked her is at large. And whoever attacked her risked a blizzard as much as she did. Our numbers are down, too." She meant that most people in the sheriff's department were home for Christmas. "She can be better protected at home." Cooper stood up to face Everett. "Doc, this is a dangerous situation."

Upset by this news, he quietly inquired, "You really think someone would come into the hospital?"

"I do. And they will be armed. I'm pretty sure this may be connected to the murders of the two monks."

What she didn't want to say was that, if someone came in unarmed, given low staff numbers and part-time help, they might easily slip by a police guard. Also, the animals proved a good warning system at home.

"Jesus." He whistled.

"You would help us if you'd instruct anyone who has seen Harry, and this includes the ambulance driver, not to tell anyone. They might actually keep their mouths shut if you inform them they could be in danger themselves if the perp finds out they had contact with her today." Cooper breathed in. "We're dealing with someone who is both twisted and ruthless, someone who arouses no suspicion." Cooper thought to herself that Everett had no idea how ruthless.

"I'll see to it." Everett compressed his lips, then turned to his friend. "Keep her quiet."

The ambulance crawled on the way back to the farm. The snowplows worked, but there weren't enough of them to adequately deal with the weather. Virginia, blessed with four distinct seasons, benefited from mild winters compared to Maine. But winter did arrive, and Crozet rested near the foot of the Blue Ridge Mountains, so it was colder there. Often the mountains and the close foothills got more snow than even Charlottesville.

Fair sat next to Harry, as Cooper followed in her squad car. Her feet felt like ice blocks since her pants and socks remained wet. The department allowed the officers to take their vehicles home. Cooper used the car for work, obviously, but when Fair had called, suspecting trouble, she prudently drove over in the squad car. She talked to Rick as she drove.

"We don't have anyone to spare to set up a guard."

"I know, boss. I'll take turns with Fair. By December twenty-sixth, we might be able to round someone up or maybe I can find personal security. Fair will spare no expense."

"Harry won't stand for it."

"Yeah, I'm afraid of that myself. I don't know who's out there and I don't usually worry. I mean, we deal with thieves, con men, assault and batteries all the time, plus the occasional murder, usually fueled by alcohol or infidelity, but this — this is different. And I'm scared."

"I know what you mean. I don't think the killer is going to come after her, but we sure could find ourselves surprised."

"Yeah, I know. I think this is someone who is acceptable to the community, someone we see most every day," she replied.

Rick sighed. "Yeah. We're lucky Harry didn't have her throat slit." He stopped.

"I think the storm saved her. That and Mrs. Murphy and Tucker." Cooper had already told him about the animals.

"Could be right. Keep me posted."

She clicked off, concentrating on the faint taillights in front of her. Initially, she'd been disappointed when Lorenzo went home to Nicaragua for the holidays, but now she was glad, because she wouldn't have been able to spend much time with him. She liked him — more than liked him — cherishing every moment they could be together. He'd be with her for New Year's. That was a happy thought.

In the ambulance, Harry finally regained full consciousness. She tried to sit up, but Fair gently kept her down.

"Where am I?" Then she put her hand to her head, wincing, feeling the tight stitches on the part of her scalp that was shaved.

"On the way home."

"I think I'm going to be sick."

"Here." He held a plastic bag for her, since Everett had told him she might well throw up.

She did. Not much to it except excruciating pain. She flopped back on the gurney. "I've never felt so bad in my life."

"Keep quiet, honey. You'll feel much better tomorrow."

"What happened?"

"You got hit over the head. Can you tell me

why you were up there?"

She whispered with her eyes closed, as if that would diminish the pain: "At least one hundred thousand dollars in a green tool-box."

He held her hand. "That's enough for now. Do you think you can sleep?"

"Maybe. I'm dizzy."

"Can you see clearly?"

"I can see you. Looks white out the back ambulance window."

"Blizzard. Sleep, sweetie."

She conked out again. He held his palm to her forehead. She was sweating a little, but he couldn't discern a fever. A concussion doesn't bring on a fever, but the vet in him made him want to check everything.

Once at the farm, the ambulance driver and his assistant rolled Harry into the bedroom and gently placed her on the bed. She awoke, then fell back to sleep again as all three animals sat quietly on the floor.

Fair gave the two men a one-hundred-dollar tip, reminded them to say nothing, and then wished them a merry Christmas.

With Cooper's help, they got Harry out of the hospital shift, slid her under the covers, and walked back to the living room.

"Cooper, you go on home. I don't think anyone is going to invade the farm in a blizzard, and Tucker will sure let me know if anyone does."

Cooper sank into a wing chair and thought about this. "I'll be over in the morning to take a turn. I don't even trust leaving her alone while you do the barn chores."

Relief flooded his face. "Thanks, pal."

Tears formed in both their eyes again, a combination of recognizing what a near miss this was, pure physical exhaustion, and wondering what in the hell would happen next.

Cooper now struggled to get up from her chair.

"She told me there was about one hundred thousand dollars in a toolbox up there."

Cooper dropped back down. "Damn!"

"Why the hell leave it by the walnut stand —" He stopped himself. "I think I know. Some of the monks know that stand. It belonged to Susan's uncle. They may have seen it when they checked timber growth with him. And I expect there were some hard feelings when he didn't leave it to the brotherhood, the old brotherhood."

"Money can sure bring out the worst in people. The walnut stand isn't all that far from the monastery." Cooper rubbed her forehead with her right hand. "Ten thousand dollars on your kitchen table. How that money got here is anyone's guess, but if

Harry says there was a cornucopia up the mountain, then you know there was."

"I brought the money." Tucker looked at them with her deep-brown eyes.

Fair reached out to pet the silky head. "I hope whoever hit her doesn't know we have some of the money."

Cooper shrugged. "No way to tell."

"Well, we know one thing more than we did yesterday: the finger points to the top of the mountain."

"Yes, it does. Well, let me get home. And let's hope the power doesn't go off or there will be pipes bursting all over central Virginia."

"You've got a generator?"

"Do. Hooked up just in case."

"Good."

She pushed herself up once again. At the kitchen door, Fair hugged Cooper and kissed her on the cheek.

"I can never repay you, Coop."

"That's what friends are for." She hugged him back. When she put on her coat, they both noticed some blood on the back. Fair's coat also had blood drippings. They'd been too distracted to notice before now. "I'll pay for the dry-cleaning bill."

"Fair, no."

She called when she made it home.

Fair stoked the fire. Next he warmed special food for the animals, because they had braved this storm, too. He owed them as much as he owed Cooper.

Then he stripped and took a hot shower, which almost got the chill out of his bones, and he stoked the fire one more time. He wanted to crawl in bed with Harry, but he was afraid if he turned in the night or bumped her, he'd hurt her. He pulled out four blankets, put two on the floor at the foot of the bed, two over him, and used one pillow. The three animals cuddled with him. He fell asleep the minute his head hit the pillow.

Miraculously, the power stayed on.

23

Faint light shone through the windows at seven-thirty on Christmas Eve morning. Harry reached over for Fair, touched empty space, and quickly sat up. The cut on her scalp hurt. Her head throbbed.

She tiptoed to where Fair, sound asleep, was spread out. Tucker, Mrs. Murphy, and Pewter snuggled with him.

She put her finger to her lips. Tucker knew that signal. Harry went into the bathroom and tried to look at her scalp in the mirror. The blood had been washed from the wound, but a little had seeped afterward. Since the wound was on the back of her head, she couldn't see it. She picked up a washrag, wet it, and pressed it to the wound. Stung like the devil. Tears sprang up, but she kept the warm washrag there, then rinsed it out. She brushed her teeth, quite grateful that she was no longer dizzy or nauseated when she bent over. She had to laugh at her "do" and figured she'd be wearing baseball hats until the hair grew over the shaved wound.

Completing her morning ablutions, she threw on a terry bathrobe and went into the living room to rekindle the fire. The deep ash bed contained a layer of bright orange embers once she stirred it, so getting the fire up took no time at all.

Mrs. Murphy padded in. *"How do you feel?"*

Harry scooped up the cat, kissing her cheeks. "I don't know how either of us got down the mountain, Murphy, but I'm so glad we're home."

Tucker and Pewter walked in.

"Carried you down. You can't believe how hard Fair and Cooper worked," Pewter informed her. *"I've never been so cold in my life."*

"You say that every time the thermometer dips below freezing," Mrs. Murphy teased her.

"This was worse." Pewter hoped something good would soon appear in the kitchen.

"It was. I'm a little stiff today. And still a little tired," Tucker admitted.

"Small wonder." Mrs. Murphy put her paws around Harry's neck.

"Come on." Harry, her knees hurting although she didn't know why, walked into the kitchen to make a hot breakfast for all of them.

Her knees hurt because she had fallen curled up, knees bent. Harry, rarely incapacitated, was surprised when anything ached.

As she looked out the window over the sink, she was greeted by a magical land of pure white, dotted with bare trees and enlivening evergreens, boughs bent with snow. Flakes still fell, a light but steady drift. The clouds were low, medium to dark gray.

She knew she'd gone up the mountain; she was trying to remember why.

She was smart enough to know she'd suffered a concussion and grateful that she perceived no ill effect other than the thumping cut on her head. Her vision was fine. She had a dim memory of throwing up in a plastic bag in the ambulance, but her stomach now felt normal. She gave a silent prayer of thanks.

Frying some leftover hamburger for the animals, she pulled out another cast-iron skillet, rubbed it with butter, and put it on a cold burner. She intended to make scrambled eggs. When she put down the mix of warm hamburger and dry food, the three animals went crazy with delight. Made her happy to see them so happy.

Fair appreciated good coffee. She opened the freezer to grab a bag of ground beans. The others were whole-bean. She liked making coffee, even though she didn't like drinking it. Once the coffee was put up, she plugged in the electric teapot and dropped a good old Lipton's bag in a cup. She began mixing ingredients in a smallish Corning Ware bowl. Then she'd wake Fair.

Harry looked around her kitchen as though seeing it for the first time. Free of unnecessary adornment, her home reflected her in so many ways. She noticed the pegs by the door, coats hanging, a long bench with a lid underneath, boots within. A sturdy farmer's table sat in the center of the room, and there was random-width heart pine on the floor, worn thin in places of high traffic by close to two hundred years of feet and paws.

A burst of love for her life, this kitchen, the farm, and, above all, her husband, friends, and animal friends, welled up. She didn't know why she'd been hit. She felt lucky to be alive. She was determined to get to the bottom of it. She also decided to carry her .38. Thank God for the Second Amendment.

The teapot whistled and Harry shook her head at herself. Here she was trying to be quiet, but she'd forgotten about the whistle.

Fair, hearing the piercing note, awoke, feeling refreshed. Sleeping on the floor often made his back feel better. He smelled the coffee and rushed into the kitchen.

Harry laughed when her naked husband rushed into the kitchen, the floor cold on his bare feet. "Honey, put your robe on before you turn blue."

He hugged her. "Are you all right?"

"Actually, I am, but my head stings. It's pretty tender."

He kissed her. "Thank God that's all. I was afraid your skull had been cracked, but the X-rays and MRI proved what I have always known: you're very hardheaded."

She kissed him back. "Big surprise. Now go put your clothes on before you catch your death. Not that I don't like seeing you in your birthday suit. You're an impressive specimen, you know."

"If you say so." Fair had not one scrap of vanity, unusual for so well-built and handsome a man.

He finally did go put on slippers. His had fox masks embroidered on the toes. The terry-cloth robe felt good against his skin. By the time he returned to the kitchen — his teeth brushed, his hands washed, hair combed — breakfast was on the table.

Admiring the snowscape, they chatted.

Fair avoided the obvious subject until he was on his second cup of coffee, she on her second cup of tea.

"Honey, how did you wind up on the mountain?"

The reason started to come back to her. "I came home from errands and Tucker and Mrs. Murphy were missing. When they finally came back, Tucker dropped a packet with ten thousand dollars on the floor. Put on my coat and hat and followed Tucker, who was dying to lead me somewhere. Well, on and on we went, and finally, at the walnut grove, Tucker and Mrs. Murphy led me to the low rock outcropping. Fair, there was at least a hundred thousand dollars in a green toolbox! I couldn't believe it. That's all I remember."

"Brother George hit her on the head with the butt of a pistol," Tucker informed them.

"Don't waste your breath," Pewter noted.

Fair then told her his part of the story. Harry got out of her chair, hugged and kissed the two cats and the dog. She stayed on the floor for a while, Fair finally joining her to play with and praise the animals.

"Cold down here," Fair remarked.

"You know, I'd like to finally build a fireplace in the kitchen. There's an old covered-up flue where Grandma hooked up the wood-burning stove. Might still work."

"Might not work, but we'll try. I've been thinking that if we turned the screened-in porch into an extension of the kitchen, a big step-down fireplace could be built at the end. Fieldstone."

"That would be beautiful."

And behind it we could build another screened-in porch. It's nice to sit there when the weather's good. Pleasure without the mosquitoes."

"It will be expensive."

He shrugged. "Can't take it with you."

Given her close brush with eternity, she nodded. "Let me call Coop and thank her." She rose. "Not that I can ever thank her or these guys." She smiled down at Mrs. Murphy, Pewter, and Tucker. "Did Pewter really go all the way up there with you?"

"I did!" Pewter stood on her hind legs.

"Every step of the way. Poor Tucker, she fought her way up and down that mountain three times yesterday," Fair remarked.

"Well, the first time the weather wasn't bad. After that, well, I . . ." Tucker said no more.

"And, Mrs. Murphy, you stayed with me the whole time. I'd have a frostbitten nose without you."

Murphy rubbed against her leg.

As Harry walked over to the old wall

phone, Fair advised, "I know you'll want to talk to Susan, but don't. Not yet."

"Why? I tell Susan everything. Well, almost everything."

"Whoever hit you probably thinks you're dead. Given this blizzard, it's possible he thinks you haven't been found. But it's Christmas Eve, so we have two days, thanks to the weather and the holiday, where your disappearance not being in the news isn't strange. If there isn't something in the papers on Boxing Day" — Fair referred to the December 26 holiday that was celebrated by some people in the country — "then he'll know you're alive. And then" — he breathed deeply — "we can't take any chances."

"I'm not. I'm carrying my thirty-eight."

He shook his head. "Not enough. Someone is going to be with you twenty-four hours a day."

She knew enough not to argue, plus she felt a shiver of fear. "Not in bed with us, I hope."

He came right back at her. "You know, we never tried that. Any candidates?"

She punched him on the arm and picked up the phone. She reached Cooper on her landline, so the connection was clear.

"Harry!" Cooper's voice was jubilant. "You sound like yourself."

"I am, except for the clunk on the head. Thank you. Thank you a thousand times over, and am I glad I got you a good Christmas present."

Cooper laughed. "You could paint a rock. I'd be happy."

"You say. But really, Coop, I don't know how you two got me down from the walnut stand with the winds and the blowing snow. It's still snowing."

"Found out how strong I am, and Fair's stronger. I'm just so glad you're all right. Wow. What a gust. This thing isn't over. It's snowing hard now. My house is shaking."

Harry, hearing and feeling it, too, replied, "That must have been a sixty-mile-an-hour gust."

"Can you tell me what happened?"

Harry repeated to her what she'd told Fair as he washed the dishes. "I don't remember anything after that."

"If something should occur to you, call me. I'll be over to help Fair with the horses, too."

"I will." Harry felt another blast, plus the cold air seeping through cracks here and there. "Got enough firewood?"

"Yep. I watched the Weather Channel. Doesn't look like this will let up until late afternoon."

"Hard on the store owners. It will keep everyone at home."

Not quite.

24

Many families gather together on December 24, go to vespers for the traditional Christmas Eve service, return home for a late supper, and then open gifts. Others go to Christmas Eve service but wait until Christmas morning to open presents.

Despite the weather, the Reverend Jones held the St. Luke's service, attended mostly by those who could walk through the snow or who drove 4×4 vehicles. Even though attendance was low, Herb enjoyed the special event. Two enormous poinsettias, flaming red, graced the altar. Red and white poinsettias filled the vestibule, too. The glow of candles added to the soft beauty of the night service.

Dr. Bryson and Racquel Deeds made it, as did Bill and Jean Keelo. Susan and Ned Tucker attended. They lived not far from St. Luke's. Susan had carried her shoes while walking in her boots, Ned teasing her as they

plowed through the snow. Once at church, she left her boots in the cloakroom and laughed to see the rows of boots, other women making the same choice she did. She was happy that her son, now out of college, and her daughter, still attending, had accompanied her.

Alicia and BoomBoom, although living farther out, took this as an opportunity to test the Land Cruiser. Worked like a treat.

The cats entered the church's back entrance with Herb at 6:30 P.M. The service was at 7:00 P.M. Lucy Fur, Elocution, and Cazenovia sat off to the side where they could view the congregation. Cazenovia, tempted to scoot under the altar, decided against it, since she'd be peeping out from under the embroidered altar covering. She wanted to see everything but knew her poppy would either laugh or be furious. She felt she was a good Lutheran cat, but Reverend Jones didn't always see things her way.

She remarked, *"Racquel is cool to Bryson."*

Lucy Fur looked at them. *"Even has her shoulder turned away from him."*

Elocution, tail curled around her paws as she sat straight up, evidenced scant interest in the Deedses' marriage. *"Good thing we aren't Catholic. They have midnight Mass for Christmas. Roads will be even worse then."*

She couldn't see out the large stained-glass window.

Afterward, when Susan finally got home, she called Harry.

"Beautiful service."

"Always is."

"Can you believe it's still snowing?" Susan sipped on a delicious hot hard cider that Ned handed her.

"It's been so many years without a white Christmas, without enough snow, that I'm glad for it." Harry added, "Helps keep the bug population down come summer."

Harry wanted to tell her best friend about what had happened, but she kept her mouth shut.

"You know, the entire choir made it. That was a big surprise."

"What about the congregation?" Harry was curious.

"About half. Made it more intimate. Brother Luther came, which surprised me. They have their own service."

"He was raised a Lutheran — plus his name, you know."

Susan laughed. "Let's hope the original Luther displayed more personality than Brother Luther."

"Dour," Harry agreed. "The rest of them seem cheerful enough, or they were."

"Don't think I'd be too happy being one of the brothers right now." She switched subjects. "Feels like I haven't seen you in eons."

"I know. But this time of year is crazy enough, and when you add the weather, it's amazing anything gets done. Susan, do me a favor. Don't tell anyone you've spoken to me. I'll explain later."

Brother George, not happy that Brother Luther drove down the mountain in the first place, complained, "You'd better get your ass back up here by midnight. We have our own service, you know."

"I'm on my way now. You'll be pleased to know that Bill Keelo, overflowing with Christmas spirit, made a generous donation to our order. I knew if I went to St. Luke's service, I'd see him."

Brother George's tone became warm. "Good. Much as we appreciate Bill's legal work for the order, coins help. Liquid assets, Brother Luther, liquid assets. You as treasurer understand how vital they are more than anyone else."

"Do. Well, I'll be up there in an hour or so. Slow going, but it's going."

"How much, by the way?"

"Ten thousand dollars. Bill handed me an

envelope and I didn't open it until he was back in the Jeep. But he did say that he knew we'd lost business at the Christmas tree farm from being closed two whole days, so he hoped this would help us."

"How thoughtful." Brother George's voice crackled a little on the cell. "I'm losing you. See you soon."

Soon was an hour and a half later. Brother Morris met Brother Luther at the door, thanking him for the foresight to see Bill Keelo at the Christmas Eve service.

"Called ahead." Brother Luther smiled slightly.

"Yes, yes, sometimes it takes a gentle prod." Brother Morris winked, then headed to his quarters to rest before the service.

As Brother Luther headed to his own quarters, he passed Brother Sheldon, hands in his long sleeves. The hallway was cold.

"Your hands must be cold," Brother Luther said.

"Everything is cold. I wish you'd told me you were going down the mountain. I would have liked to go to St. Luke's service. It's such a pretty church."

"Ah, well, next time."

"Next time is a year away."

"Sheldon, maybe by then you'll stop crying at the drop of a hat."

Brother Sheldon's face flushed crimson. "We've lost two good young men."

"Yes, we have, but you can be glad of one thing."

"Which is?" Brother Sheldon glared at Brother Luther.

"At least it wasn't you."

At midnight, Racquel called the sheriff's department. After St. Luke's, Bryson had dropped her off at home and said he was going to see if the convenience store was open, as they needed milk. They didn't. She'd checked the fridge the minute she walked inside the house.

Furious, she called on his cell, but he didn't pick up. She was beyond suspicion that he was having an affair. Now she just knew it. How stupid was he to leave his wife and family on Christmas Eve? She thought he'd be back in an hour. He wasn't back by midnight.

She reported him as a missing person and devoutly prayed he'd be picked up if his SUV had slid off the road, or perhaps an officer would cruise by the house of whomever he was sleeping with, to find his vehicle in the driveway, a mantle of snow already covering where he'd cleaned it off.

Still, she couldn't believe he'd be stupid enough to do this on Christmas Eve.

What was his game?

25

When Officer Doak received the call from the dispatcher, he was driving back from a wreck on I-64. Some fool, filled with good cheer and in a nice Nissan Murano, had disregarded the treacherous conditions, only to sail through a guardrail and down an embankment. The loaded twenty-six-year-old bank teller didn't even have a scratch. The Murano was totaled.

Much as Officer Doak wished he wasn't working on Christmas Eve and now early Christmas morning, he knew Rick would be taking over at four. The sheriff had many good qualities as a leader, one of his strongest being that he would pull duty on days when others really wanted to be with their families. Rick and Helen had no children. Their parents still lived, so they'd visit both sets over the holidays. However, Rick often worked during a holiday, feeling those people with children needed to be home. If the boss worked in the middle of the night on Christmas, no one in the department could complain about their schedule.

So Doak cruised slowly in his squad car. All the people in the department had special driving training, which paid off on nights such as this.

Racquel, wide awake and still dressed in her Christmas best, greeted him at the door. The boys, both teenagers, slept, unaware.

Once in the kitchen, far away from the stairs up to the second floor, Racquel filled him in on the time frame of the evening.

"A navy-blue 2008 Tahoe with Jamestown plates." He checked the number on the plates, which she'd provided for him.

Officer Doak marveled at her coolness, her ability to supply necessary information. "This has been going on for six months. Late calls, emergencies at the hospital." She tapped a painted fingernail on the hard surface of the table. "Not that there aren't emergencies for a cardiologist, but let's just say there was always one too many. We've been married eighteen years. I know the drill as well as he does."

"Yes, ma'am."

"Could I offer you a Christmas drink?"

"Oh, no, thank you, ma'am. Can't drink on duty."

"Coffee?"

"No, thank you. Do you have any idea where he might be?"

"No. At first I thought it was one of the nurses, but I've seen the nurses. I think not," she said in a clipped tone. "But when doctors stray, they usually do so in the confines of the hospital. It's a closed world, a hothouse."

"Yes, ma'am." He stood. "I'll be on the lookout for a navy-blue Tahoe."

"The one thing that keeps me from picking up a shotgun and going after him myself is that it's Christmas Eve — well, Christmas. I simply can't believe he'd pull a stunt like this on Christmas."

"Yes, ma'am." Officer Doak politely took his leave.

He had two and a half hours remaining. He'd planned to go back to headquarters. With the exception of the one drunk on I-64, there wasn't any traffic. Usually the state police handled I-64, and they had arrived a half hour after Doak. He was close by, so he hadn't minded heading to the Deedses' house when he heard the call. For one thing, it staved off boredom and loneliness.

Being unmarried and still under thirty, Officer Doak tried to imagine what he'd do if he were having an affair. If the woman was unmarried herself, he could go to her house, but most people would be with their families. Many people from other places would have been taken in by locals. No one should be alone on Christmas Eve and Christmas.

If it was a quick rendezvous, he supposed they could park under the football or soccer stadium, in a parking lot that was hidden. He slowly circled the university holdings on the west side of business Route 29. Didn't see a thing except snow.

He rounded by the law school, part of a series of buildings erected from the '70s onward and sadly out of character with the core of the University of Virginia. Not that they were butt ugly. The shape and proportion of the Darden School and the law school might have even been welcome in many a Midwestern university, but not here, where things should have been built in Mr. Jefferson's style. Jefferson, could he have seen the new additions, would have suffered cardiac arrest.

Officer Doak's heart ticked fine, but he possessed enough aesthetic sense to recognize a mistake — a quite expensive one, too — when he saw it.

Driving out of the university, he came up behind Barracks Road Shopping Center, which was still central to economic life in Charlottesville. The windshield wipers clicked as he turned into the center. One lone snow-covered car reposed in the parking lot in front of Barnes & Noble, which was a real gathering spot during business hours.

He drove up, got out, wiped off the license plates to be sure. It was Dr. Bryson Deeds's Tahoe, all right. He wiped off a window. No one was inside.

Snow fell on his nose. He pulled his cap down tighter around his head, but it offered little by way of warmth. He climbed back into the squad car, his feet already cold. He drove along the main row of buildings. Even with the overhang, the winds swept snow inward. He passed the small fountain areas and noticed a lone figure wearing a Santa Claus hat sitting on a bench. He kept the motor running, got out, and identified Bryson, throat cleanly sliced.

Doak immediately called Rick.

The minute the sheriff heard Doak's voice, he was wide awake. "What?"

"Dr. Bryson Deeds is dead. M.O. like the monks."

"I'll be right there."

Rick arrived in fifteen minutes. He lived up the hill behind Barracks Road but drove cautiously. "Thank God no one's around."

"Right," Doak replied.

Rick wished he'd put on more layers. "Until the coroner examines the corpse, we can't assume it's the same killer."

"Copycat?"

"Possible. The variation in this murder is that Bryson is not a monk."

Officer Doak informed him of Racquel's call and his visit to the house.

Rick had called the ambulance squad and managed to rouse one person from the forensics team, since the rest were out of town. He checked his watch.

"Should I go back to his wife?"

"Not yet. You're off duty in an hour. I'll do it."

The young man blew air from his cheeks. "Thanks, Chief. I hate that."

"I do, too, but sometimes you can pick up useful information."

Officer Doak looked at Bryson's corpse and said, "Arrogant bastard."

"Could be, but he was also one of the best cardiologists on the Atlantic seaboard. I expect his fan club consisted of those he'd saved and few others. Is the Tahoe unlocked?"

"Didn't check."

Rick pushed his coat sleeve back to check

the time again. "The coroner will have to take a crowbar to pry him off the bench."

Neither of them could help it — they laughed a little.

"Want me to go through the Tahoe?"

"In a minute."

The young man folded his arms across his chest, stamped his feet a little. "Coop and I were talking about the murders. The killer believes he's unassailable, which could be dangerous."

Rick nodded. "Anyone that arrogant, if pinned down, will try to kill again."

"Or hire an expensive lawyer."

"Maybe," Rick said, then continued, "but I've been a cop long enough to know that whoever is doing this has a gargantuan ego. The offense to that ego of being outsmarted by a 'dumb cop' like me or you or Coop, I'm telling you, is going to make the son of a bitch snap."

26

It was a long night on top of Afton Mountain.

After the simple Christmas Eve service infused with Gregorian chants, the brothers wished one another the compliments of the season and most retired to their cells. A few intended to enter into the spirit of the holiday. Bottles were liberated from safe places, with toasts quietly lifted to the order, to increased happiness, and, of course, to the departed.

Brother Morris asked Brother George to share a libation with him. The two men sat on a comfortable sofa. Brother Morris could take only so much denial of creature comforts. Given his girth, a supportive place to park was more than understandable, as was the heating pad on which he placed his aching feet. With the bulk they supported, it was a wonder he wasn't crippled.

"Merry Christmas, George." He lifted his glass.

George lifted his glass of excellent scotch. "The same to you, Brother."

"Can this place be any more beautiful than it has been these last two days with the snow falling? The red cardinal sat on the outstretched hand of the statue of the Blessed Virgin Mother. A slash of color against pristine white." Brother Morris savored the Johnnie Walker Blue Label. "Somehow it is easier to go without the enticements of modern life when one is surrounded by such beauty."

"Yes, it is. Can't help it, though, my mind goes back to my childhood Christmases. Usually snowed in Maine. We had a lot of fun."

"Your sisters will carry on the tradition."

"All except for getting dead drunk." Brother George laughed.

"I'm glad we have this quiet time together. I went over the books last night."

Brother George snorted. "Brother Luther will take offense. He balances those books to the penny."

"No, not those books. *Our* books."

"Oh." Brother George's sharp features changed, a feral alertness crept into his face.

"We're missing ten thousand dollars. What happened?"

Uncharacteristically, Brother George

gulped his entire drink, then poured another, knowing full well that a bottle of Johnnie Walker Blue skated close to two hundred dollars a pop. "Yes, well, I was going to tell you about that after Christmas. No point in ruining a holiday."

"Tell me now." Brother Morris oozed warmth and understanding.

"Well, it's a little embarrassing."

"George, are you gambling again?" This, too, was asked with warmth.

"No, no. I'll never do that."

"Then tell me. Ten thousand dollars is a pleasing sum, pleasing in the eyes of the Lord." Morris smiled broadly.

"The money was right where it was supposed to be. I got there just as the storm broke, and . . . uh" — Brother George stared deep into his glass for guidance — "and Harry Haristeen was bending over the toolbox. It was open, and I hit her over the head with my gun, took the box, and ran. Plus that damned dog of hers was there, and I'm scared of dogs."

Astonished, Brother Morris first sputtered, "It's just a corgi, you fool."

"All dogs bite."

His composure returning, Brother Morris, not radiating warmth now, said, "Yes, of course, how brave of you to face death from the ankles down."

"It's not funny. Dogs terrify me."

"Did you search Harry for the money?"

"Hell, no. I ran for all I was worth."

"How hard did you hit her?" Brother Morris needed a second scotch himself.

"Hard enough to coldcock her."

"And the blizzard was starting?"

"Yes." Brother George's voice betrayed his nervousness.

"And you left her there!"

"What else could I do? She didn't see me. The winds were howling. I'd come up from behind. The dog barked, and the cat was there, too."

"Scratch your eyes out, I'm sure. Let me get this straight. You found one of Crozet's leading citizens bent over the toolbox. You hit her on the head with your gun?"

"The butt of the gun." Brother George was specific.

"All right. She was unconscious and you left. Did you call an ambulance later?"

"No. How could I do that?"

Brother Morris's face turned red. "From a phone, not yours, and you can disguise your voice." He lowered his to a belligerent whisper. "She might be frozen to death. Jesus Christ. Murder! Two of our most productive brothers have been heinously killed and now this. Are you out of your mind?"

"No, but I panicked. I could go down to her farm tomorrow. I could check around."

"Idiot!" Brother Morris raised his voice, which even at a stage whisper could carry unmiked.

Brother George sank farther into the sofa. "I'm sorry. I am truly sorry. What can I do?"

"How about the Stations of the Cross?" Brother Morris sarcastically cited a ritual of deep penance.

"I don't even know what they are."

"Some Catholic you are."

"I'm not a Catholic. I'm a Methodist, and you know it."

"The Methodist Church has a lot to answer for if you're a product."

Helplessly, Brother George pleaded, "What do you want me to do?"

"Nothing. Nothing." He uttered the second "nothing" softly. "I'll take care of it."

"Maybe I could drum up a contribution to make up what I lost?"

Brother Morris stared at him as though he were five years old with an ice-cream cone about to drip on the sofa.

"Forget it."

"I could go to Bryson for money."

"No. Anyway, he's made a contribution, and that is Brother Luther's job."

"Maybe Racquel would like to give something. We could put her name on something." Brother George was desperate. "When I stopped by his office, Bryson mentioned that Racquel is interested in what we do. He also mentioned that she thinks he's having an affair. He was a little worried. His marriage is important to him."

"Given the social status she brings him — old blood — I guess it is. Listen to me. The money is gone. Ten thousand dollars isn't worth you making a bigger mess of things. I seriously doubt Racquel would give us money, especially if she doubts her husband and we are his main charity, not her."

"Actually, I think he loves her."

Brother Morris shrugged. "Perhaps. I've never been able to untangle love from dependency. She all but wipes his ass for him." A hint of venom escaped Brother Morris's lips.

"I've let you down. Please let me make it up."

"At this point, you'd screw up a two-car funeral. Do nothing. Say nothing. Well, you can pray."

"Yes. I've grown to like praying."

"Then get on your knees and pray that Harry Haristeen isn't dead. If she is, there will be hell to pay."

"But no one knows I hit her."

"Not now and maybe not ever, but murder is a terrible crime. You know" — he wiggled his toes on the heating pad — "so many of the operas I've sung involved the consequences of dreadful deeds. I believe it."

"Yes, well." Brother George never thought of himself as a murderer.

"And we are under scrutiny because of the deaths of Brother Christopher and Brother Speed. We can't afford a misstep. When the sheriff or his deputy come back, make yourself scarce. I don't trust that you won't give yourself away."

"I won't say anything. I know you think I'm an idiot, but I'm not that stupid."

"It's not what you say. It's how you act. Don't give them a chance to read you."

"I'll try." He then asked, "I do wonder who killed those two. They were lovely men. Lovely."

"If I ever get my hands on who did it, I'll risk going to jail myself." He looked at Brother George. "Perhaps there was no other way to retrieve the money. She wouldn't have left it there, but to leave a woman in the snow, in the cold, a storm brewing — Goddamnit, the least you could have done was call someone. Me, for instance."

"I panicked. I told you, all I thought of was protecting our interests."

Wearily, Brother Morris said, "Leave me. Don't worry. I'm not going to make you suffer. George, you made a mistake, let's leave it at that."

After Brother George slunk away, Brother Morris killed the bottle of Johnnie Walker Blue.

27

"You are too much!" Susan threw open the kitchen door and yelled.

Harry, in the living room, contemplating wrapping paper strewn all over the floor, heard her best friend's voice. "So are you!"

They collided in the kitchen with the hugs, kisses, and usual screams of Southern women who adored each other and had been apart anywhere from twenty-four hours to twenty-four years.

"Where's handsome?"

"In the barn. One of my Christmas presents was that he would do all the chores. Did them yesterday, too. Want to feed Simon and the owl with me? They get Christmas treats." Harry wore a baseball cap to cover her wound.

"Sure." Susan walked into the living room. "I can see your crew has had a big Christmas."

"Tearing up the paper — that's okay. It's

when they climb the tree that there's a prob-lem." Harry surveyed the scene, deciding the hell with it. "I love my present."

"Love mine, too. Whatever possessed you to buy me a rotisserie?"

"Whatever possessed you to buy me a vac-uum for the horses?"

At this they burst out laughing, realizing that for the last year each of them had re-peatedly mentioned how much the rotisserie and the vacuum would ease their respective chores.

"What'd your honey-do husband get you?"

Susan clapped her hands together. "He bought me season tickets to the Virginia Theater in Richmond and a day at the spa, but, best of all, look!" She held out her right arm, on which dangled an intricately wrought bracelet of eighteen-karat gold. "Can you believe? At today's prices, no less."

"That's gorgeous." Harry held Susan's arm, pretending to unlock the bracelet.

Susan slapped her hand. "How about you?"

"A huge thermos so I can make his coffee the nights he's on call. He says I need my sleep and, much as he loves me getting up to hand him a thermos, he wants me to sleep. There's the thermos." She pointed under the tree. "I mean, you could water a platoon with that."

"He'll need both hands to carry it. What else?" Susan's eyebrows raised expectantly.

"A necklace to match the ring he bought me last summer when we visited the Shelbyville Saddlebred show." Harry knelt down, lifting up a luxurious presentation box. "Look at this."

"Spectacular. He really does have good taste."

"But here's the best present of all. I can't believe he bought me one." She breathed in deeply, as if to contain her excitement. "A Honda ATV. I mean, this thing is four hundred horsepower. And, thank God, he didn't buy one in camouflage. It's a pleasing shade of blue. I can go seventy miles an hour on it if I want and through anything."

"If you go seventy miles an hour on that beast, I will beat your ass with a wooden spoon. Where is it?"

"In the shed. Come on." Harry walked back to the kitchen, pulled a coat off the peg.

Susan, who'd thrown her coat on a kitchen chair, zipped it back up. As Harry tried to slide the baseball cap down against the weather, Susan noticed the edge of the nasty cut, plus some bare scalp.

"Hey. What'd you do?"

"Oh, a little accident."

"Bullshit, Harry." Susan snatched the Orioles cap off her head. "Stitches. Whoever did it was careful to shave just around the wound. But, girl, you need help. Better call Glen at West Main." She cited a fashionable hair salon.

"I clunked my head on a beam."

"None of your beams are that low." Susan folded her arms across her chest. "Furthermore, I know you better than you know yourself. 'Fess up."

"I can't." Harry sounded morose.

Susan knew Harry shared most everything with her, so her conclusion was easy to reach. "You're in trouble and Rick told you to button it." She touched her lips.

"Well —"

"Harry, I know you found Christopher Hewitt. Made the papers, and you told me everything. At least I think you did."

"I did tell you. When Dr. Gibson found the obol, I told you that, too. However, Rick and Cooper let me know I had to keep quiet about this." She took the cap back, clapped it on her head, then walked out onto the screened-in porch.

Susan, hot on her tail, said, "Listen, I don't want to have this conversation in front of Fair, but if you've stuck your nose into the two monks being killed, the killer must have found out."

"I haven't. I *swear* I haven't."

"Then who hit you on the head hard enough to split it open like that?"

"I don't know. He — or she, but I think he — came up behind me as the blizzard started."

"On the farm? That person came here?" Susan was aghast.

"No." Harry slipped her arm through Susan's as she opened the screen door. "I can't tell you any more, even though I'm dying to."

"It's the dying I'm worried about. Is that why you didn't want me to tell anyone I'd talked to you?"

"Yes." Harry walked slowly as they navigated the cleared path, now turned to ice. "Forgot the treats. Wait a minute."

She carefully walked back to the house, pulled out a small Tupperware full of mince pie, and grabbed molasses icicles from the freezer and a bag of marshmallows from the pantry.

On returning, she handed the Tupperware to Susan. "Now, if we hold hands, we'll be in balance. We each have something to carry with the other."

"Sure." Susan smiled at her.

"And, Susan, I'm not scared much, but I'm scared enough. No point in pretending otherwise to you."

"What kind of person would show up in a snowstorm? A desperate one, I think."

"I don't know. But if it is Christopher's or Brother Speed's killer, why didn't he kill me?"

"I don't know, but I'm exceedingly grateful."

They entered the barn, the horses nickering a greeting. Fair was sweeping up the center aisle.

"Merry Christmas." He leaned the big push broom against a stall and kissed Susan.

"Those were some presents you gave your wife."

He grinned. "Seen the Honda yet?"

"No."

"Four hundred horsepower, much of which translates into torque, as opposed to on a motorcycle. What a difference it will make on the farm, and it burns less gas than one of the trucks."

"I cleaned up this Christmas." Harry looked at the ladder to the hayloft just as Simon was looking down. "Simon, merry Christmas."

"*Goody.*" He smelled the molasses, for she'd unzipped the plastic bag.

"You wait one minute while I put out the owl's present." She handed the bag to Susan, and Susan gave her the Tupperware container. She climbed the ladder, which was flat against the wall and well secured.

On reaching the hayloft, she pulled the top off the container and put it on a high hay bale. As she turned to reach for the offered Ziploc bag from Susan, she heard a slight whoosh as the predator opened her wide wings to glide down. Harry didn't look back at the owl, letting her pick her treats in peace.

"We got good presents, too." Tucker loved gifts.

"All right, Simon, just another minute." Harry reached into the Ziploc and took the icicles from it. She also dumped the marshmallows on the loft floor.

"Think gelato started this way in ancient Rome?" Susan eyed the icicles.

"They had everything we do but without machines. They had ice, gelato, better roads than ours, interesting architecture, cooling gardens, running water. If you had money, life was sweet."

"Like today." Fair picked up the broom to finish his job.

Susan joked, "The more things change, the more they stay the same."

Simon waited a respectful distance away, but the minute Harry backed down the ladder, he grabbed one molasses icicle, eagerly devouring it. Next he selected a marshmallow.

"I got catnip. And a fleece bed." Pewter thought some attention should be paid to her.

"Me, too." Mrs. Murphy liked having her own bed.

"I got a new collar and leash and a big fleece bed." Tucker happily recounted her gifts. *"Dog bones."*

As the three humans and three animals left the barn, Cooper came down the long drive. She parked, flung open the door, and hugged Harry, then Fair.

"Merry Christmas." Fair hugged her back.

"What a great present! A power washer. I am so excited. I can clean the squad car, the outside of the house. I can't believe it."

"Oster clippers are pretty special. You conferred with Susan, didn't you?" Harry smiled as she mentioned a powerful brand of clippers favored by horsemen.

"Did."

"Come on in. We're having a party. Susan escaped the home fires for a little bit," Fair told Cooper.

"On my way to the morgue."

"Why?" All three stared at her.

"Because I'm free this Christmas. When Mom and Dad moved to New Mexico this spring, that solved the Christmas to-do. Rick has Helen, so when he called me, I told him to go home." She realized she'd said too much, as they didn't know about Bryson, so she hastened to add, "Probably one of the drunks froze at the mall. Still, I'd better check."

"You wouldn't go if it wasn't important. Has there been another murder?" Fair asked.

Cooper kept mum, which told them everything.

Susan jumped in. "Another Brother of Love?"

"Oh, all right. The family has been notified and it will be in tomorrow's paper. Bryson Deeds."

"What!" Fair exclaimed.

"Throat slit." Cooper got back in the squad car. "I'll know the rest of it after the autopsy. God bless Doc Gibson, because he came in to do this."

The corpse had been thawing since three in the morning. Dr. Gibson and Mandy Sweetwater straightened the limbs and examined the body before cutting Bryson open.

A patient soul, Dr. Gibson was a bit irritated that the dead monks' tissue samples he'd sent to the Richmond lab still hadn't been examined. Granted, it was the holiday season, but sometimes, if very lucky, a DNA sample will match one already on record.

Cooper noted what the older doctor dictated. Mandy, interning in pathology, also made a few comments.

Although Bryson's jaw was a bit tight, Dr. Gibson pried it open, retrieving an obol.

Cooper put down her notebook. She felt a nagging sense of failure. And what was the significance of the obol?

28

Boxing Day, December 26, was one of Harry's favorite days. Both Harry and Fair, accustomed to early rising, watched the eastern sky send out slivers of gray, which brightened to a dark periwinkle blue with the first blush of pink outlining the horizon.

"Did you call the huntline?" Fair, groggy until a huge coffee mug was placed before him, asked.

"Honey, I did last night before we went to bed. There's no Boxing Day hunt, because many of the secondary and tertiary roads remain unplowed. Also, the footing will be so deep in spots, we'd have to paddle our way through."

Both foxhunted, which was prudent considering Fair's practice. They wearied of telling people not accustomed to country life that, no, the fox was not killed. Couldn't do it even if they wanted to, thanks to the animal's lightning-fast intelligence.

For any couple, sharing activities keeps the flame bright, yet each partner should have one or two activities that belong to him or her alone. That activity for Harry was growing her grapes, although Fair helped when asked. For him it was golf, a game he had taken up five years ago. Fair couldn't decide if the relaxation outweighed the frustration. Harry kept her mouth shut about it.

"Oh." He tested the coffee, still a bit too hot.

"Waffles." She heated up the portable griddle.

"You're spoiling me."

"That's the point." She flashed a grin at him. "You don't have to do the chores. I'm fine. And I'm packing my thirty-eight."

"We'll do them together. Not on call until tomorrow. Boy, it's great when I have Christmas off. So many Christmases I've been on call."

"Well, once you started swapping weekends with Greg Schmidt" — she mentioned a highly respected equine vet, and one fabulous horseman to boot — "life did pick up. I keep telling you this, but how about for a New Year's resolution: find a partner. Maybe two."

The coffee was the perfect temperature now.

Fair chugged half the big cup, then replied, "I know, I know. Give me a day to think about making that New Year's resolution."

"Okay." She poured the batter onto the griddle, the sizzle alone enticing the three extremely attentive animals on the floor.

"All right, you beggers." Fair knocked back his coffee and rose to feed Mrs. Murphy, Pewter, and Tucker.

Harry refilled his cup.

"I like my bowl better than yours." Pewter's new ceramic bowl had "Diva" in large letters around it.

"Good. Then you'll keep your fat face out of mine," Mrs. Murphy replied as she bit into her favorite beef Fancy Feast, an expensive cat food.

Tucker kept eating. That was more important than talking. Her bowl, larger than the kitties', read "Fido," for faithful. Mrs. Murphy's read "Catitude."

Fair picked up his cup, took another big swallow, then turned on the small flat-screen TV on the kitchen wall. Harry didn't like having TV in the kitchen, but once she realized that watching her beloved Weather Channel here proved more convenient than running into the bedroom, she accepted it.

Fair clicked on the early-morning local news. Before he could sit down, the somber

face of Sheriff Rick Shaw speaking from his office was intercut with clips of a snowy Barracks Road Shopping Center, empty except for the Tahoe. Then clips of Bryson's office were shown as the latest shocking murder was revealed.

Mug poised midair, Fair stood motionless.

Harry left her griddle to stand next to him. Both of them were shocked and very upset.

Fair finally spoke. "The Tahoe in the parking lot makes it . . . I don't know, real. Worse somehow."

"It's like a killing frenzy." Harry put her arm around his waist. "The other two were monks. None of us felt in danger. I thought the key was that the victims were monks."

"Guess we can all throw that key out the window." He returned to his chair, sitting with a heavy thump.

The three cohorts on the floor said nothing but had listened as intently as the humans.

Harry turned off the griddle, flipping the contents onto a big plate. The syrup and honey sat on the table along with butter, utensils, and two plates. She poured herself a second cup of tea and sat across from Fair.

"Maybe not."

Fair drenched his waffles with honey. "Maybe not what?"

"Monks may still be the key. Bryson

treated some of them, you know."

Fair cut his waffles into neat squares before spearing one. "Right. It's a wonder he didn't take out an ad in the paper to announce his pro bono work. He made sure we all knew of his charitable deeds, that being one. I never liked the man, but I didn't wish him dead, especially like this."

Tucker lifted her head and barked, *"Intruder."*

Fair rose, then went onto the porch to open the door. "Brother Morris, come right on in."

Fair, like just about every Southerner you will ever meet, acted as though this unexpected visit was the most natural thing in the world and a big treat.

Brother Morris, who hadn't worn a coat because the distance to the door from his car was short, stepped inside.

Harry had already poured his coffee. "Sit down, Brother. How good to see you."

His visit meant others would know she was alive. Susan would keep her secret until the workweek started, but she couldn't tell Brother Morris to do so.

"I apologize for dropping by without calling. Oh, thank you." She put the half-and-half and cubed sugar before him. "You know the news, I assume, since the TV's on."

"We just watched it. You mean Dr. Deeds's murder?" replied Fair, who rose to turn off the TV.

Having a TV on when a guest is in the room is considered rude in Virginia, unless they are there to watch with you.

Harry placed waffles in front of Brother Morris, who knew he should wave them away but they smelled so delicious. He weakened immediately.

"Fellows, I'm making more, so don't hold back." She turned the griddle back on and poured more batter. "Brother, what in the world is happening?"

"I don't know. Sheriff Shaw called me at six yesterday. I must pay a call to Racquel and the boys today. The Deedses have been so supportive of our order. I thought I'd stop by here first, because you're on the way but also because you know — I should say knew — Bryson in another context than I did. St. Luke's, I mean." He looked over to Harry at the counter. "I thought maybe you had some insight. I feel like I should put up barriers to the monastery."

"Unless it's someone within," Harry blurted out as Fair tried not to drop his head in his hands.

Sometimes Harry could open her mouth before weighing her words.

"Never. I'd know. Can you think of anyone or any reason?" Brother Morris didn't take offense.

"I can't. Fair and I were just discussing that."

Fair carefully placed his fork on his plate. "Whoever is doing this can't live far. How would they get to Crozet or Afton Mountain with the weather? Brother, this person may not be in your brotherhood, but it must be someone with an intimate connection."

At the word "intimate," Brother Morris raised his dark eyebrows. "I've sat with Brother George and Brother Luther, our treasurer. We've gone over the list of people who have supported us. We've even made lists of delivery people. No one jumps out at us, and no one has even had cross words with any of us. It's baffling and frightening."

"Maybe it's someone who's mentally ill." Harry flipped more waffles onto a plate.

"Perhaps." Brother Morris sounded mournful, even though he'd just inhaled two waffles.

Harry had never seen food disappear so quickly in her life, and Fair could eat a lot himself.

"I wish we did have some ideas," Fair said.

"Ah, well, it was a hope that maybe you

knew something of Bryson's character that I didn't."

"The only thing I can say about Bryson is that his exceedingly high opinion of himself grated on some people," Harry said. "But he also had some close friends, like Bill Keelo. Some people could take him and some couldn't."

"That could be said of us all."

After finishing his waffles, Brother Morris thanked them profusely, and he thanked Harry again for the pitch pipe. When he reached the door he appeared to notice Harry's deep cut for the first time as her baseball hat, a bit loose so as not to irritate the wound, slipped a little.

"Harry, what did you do to your head?"

"Low beam," she replied with half a smile.

"I thought that was something on a car," he replied, half-smiling to himself as he left.

29

The afternoon of Boxing Day, Harry, Fair, Susan, and Ned drove to Racquel's, where Jean and Bill Keelo greeted them. Jean had organized everything, from answering the phones to keeping a notebook with information of who brought food. Miranda Hogendobber placed food on the dining-room table and kept the coffee going. The place was jammed with people.

Bill Keelo and Alex Corbett made sure people had enough to eat and drink. They acted as unofficial ushers, in a sense.

Susan carried a large casserole, while Harry had made a huge plate of small sandwiches. The two Deeds teenagers had their friends there. Everyone must have realized that teenagers eat a lot, because there was enough food to feed the entire high school senior class.

After handing over the food, the next thing that the Haristeens and the Tuckers had to do was properly visit the new widow. Racquel sat by the fireplace in the living room. Tears flowed, but that was natural. Upset as she was, vanity probably saved her. What does a new widow wear? In Racquel's case it was a suede suit, a heavy gold necklace, and small domed gold earrings to match her domed ring. Flanked by her sons, who didn't quite know what to do, Racquel accepted proffered hands and kisses on the cheeks. Racquel did rise to greet Harry and Fair, Susan and Ned behind them.

"Please don't get up." Fair gently seated her.

"What was he doing at Barracks Road? What?"

No one could answer this question.

Susan bent low to say, "Racquel, I am so terribly sorry."

Ned kissed her on the cheek, while Harry and Fair shook the boys' hands and hugged them, too.

The contrast of the house — all red and gold for Christmas — with the emotional misery only underscored how awful everyone felt.

A new stream of classmates entered. Harry knew they'd be at sixes and sevens, too. It takes some time to learn how to handle these events, but the good thing was, the boys would be surrounded by their friends. In years to come, they would remember who came to console them.

Both Harry and Susan went into the kitchen, where Miranda was in command.

"Dreadful! Dreadful!" Miranda wrapped her arms around Harry, then Susan.

"Frightening." Susan began garnishing a huge plate of sliced ham with parsley.

These women had attended those who were bereaved many times. They worked hand in glove.

Harry pulled the overflowing trash bag out of the can, tightened the drawstring, and walked it out to the porch to place it in one of the large garbage cans.

On reentering the kitchen she said, "Remind me to take the trash when I go."

"Thank you, Harry. I was beginning to worry about that." Miranda deftly stacked biscuits on a plate. "There will be a few runs to the dump today."

"There's enough food here to feed an army." Harry glanced around at the incredible abundance.

"That's problem number two." Miranda kept stacking biscuits. "I don't know where to store all this food. She's going to need it."

As if on cue, the doorbell rang and another

flood of people washed through the front door. BoomBoom helped carry the largesse into the kitchen. Alicia, also burdened, followed behind her.

"Put it on the counter." Miranda pointed.

Harry went over to greet her two foxhunting buddies.

"There's enough food here to feed an army." BoomBoom unknowingly repeated Harry's sentiments after kissing her on the cheek.

"Out-of-town people will begin arriving tomorrow and for the rest of the week. We'll go through all of this," Miranda informed them.

Alicia offered, "Why can't we all take some home and then bring it back in the morning?"

"Might work. Let me check with Jean." Miranda looked up as the kitchen door swung open and yet more food arrived.

Just then Jean pushed through the door. "How are you doing, Miranda?"

"Doing," Miranda said, then told her of the distributing food idea.

"Yes, that ought to solve the problem." Jean turned to leave as the doorbell rang again and she heard Bill's voice greeting more people.

"Harry." Miranda pointed to an overflowing garbage bag.

"That was fast." Harry carried it out to the porch. Returning, she mentioned, "We need more garbage cans."

Miranda said, "I'll run by Wal-Mart. Can't do anything now."

"Ah." Harry had opened her mouth to say more when a loud voice in the living room riveted all their attention.

"I don't care!" Racquel shouted.

Harry and Susan hurried into the room to see if anything could be done.

Tom, at fifteen Racquel's oldest son, tugged at her arm. "Mom, Mom, come on."

She shook him off, then bore down once more on Brother Luther. "He's dead because of you! They're all dead because of you."

Shocked, Brother Luther took a step back. "I thought Brother Morris —"

"I was too tired to put two and two together." Her face turned as red as Christmas wrapping paper. "I can add now."

"Perhaps I should leave." Brother Luther turned and headed out of the room.

"They're all dead because of you. Because of that damned monastery! I know it."

Reverend Jones, who had been there for about fifteen minutes, leaned over to take both of Racquel's hands in his. "Let's walk for a bit." Herb was always good in situations like this.

She allowed herself to be pulled up. Tom walked with his mother. Dr. Everett Finch, a colleague of Bryson's, walked with them, as well. With some persuasion, the three managed to get her upstairs. Everett administered a sedative.

When the three men returned, the room was buzzing.

Tom joined his friends. They were shocked into silence and had the good sense to keep quiet. The adults proved another matter.

Alicia listened politely as Biddy Doswell offered her insights. "Phantoms. At first I thought the murders were committed by gnomes — you know, the ones who live underground and have mole feet and human hands." Alicia feigned fascination, so Biddy blathered on. "No, it's phantoms of the angry dead. They are taking revenge on those of us living who resemble the humans that hurt them. Phantoms never forget, you know. Why, some are even in this room now."

Finally, Alicia pulled herself away while Biddy lassoed another victim. Alicia hurried into the kitchen, the door swinging behind her.

"That bad?" BoomBoom was wrapping

food in tinfoil.

"Biddy."

"Oh," came the chorus from Miranda, BoomBoom, Harry, and Susan, who had returned to the kitchen.

"Gnomes again?" Harry, like everyone, had been bagged by Biddy to hear this theory.

"Phantoms now." Alicia stifled a laugh despite the circumstances.

"Good God." Susan threw up her hands, then asked, "What is going on up at the monastery? Maybe the phantoms are there."

"Maybe the killer is one of the monks," BoomBoom said logically.

"Could be. Bryson may have figured it out." Harry tied up yet another garbage bag. "We're going to need more of these things."

"I'll pick up some on the way home," Alicia volunteered.

"The thing is" — Susan paid no attention to the garbage bags — "something is wrong up there."

"The monks are probably making moonshine. A lucrative trade if you're good at it," BoomBoom said.

"Two monks weren't killed over moonshine. Moonshine boys know how to get even, but murder wasn't necessary. It's something we can't imagine. But what could have aroused this fury, this frenzy?" Harry hated not knowing something.

"The sheriff has been up there. Don't you think if something were out of whack, he'd notice?"

"Apparently not." BoomBoom then said, "Honey, write down who takes what. I'm going to round up the girls and have everyone take a dish or dishes. Are you ready, Miranda?"

"Until the next wagon train pulls in."

"While you all do that, let me go let Tucker out of the truck to go to the bathroom." Harry walked into the front hall and retrieved her coat. The cats had stayed home today, although not by choice. She was glad for the cold, fresh air as she walked carefully over the icy sidewalk.

Despite the rock salt on it, the ice was so thick that only patches of it had melted.

Just as Harry opened the door for Tucker, Brother George and Brother Ed pulled up.

When Brother George opened the door, Tucker attacked. *"You hit my mother!"*

"Tucker! Tucker!"

"I'll kill you."

Brother George screamed as the fangs sank through his pants. Finally Harry got the corgi off, bustling her back into the truck.

"He's the murderer! He hit you and left you in the blizzard."

She ran over to Brother George, who had pulled up his pants leg, where blood was trickling down.

"I am so sorry. I'll pay for any doctor bills. I don't know why she did that. She's never done that."

Brother George knew exactly why Tucker had attacked. "No need, no need. Given all that's happened, this is a small worry."

Brother Ed, on his knees and nearly stuck to the snow, examined the puncture wounds. "You'll be all right. Let's go inside and see if we can wash this with alcohol."

"Don't," Harry bluntly ordered them. "Racquel told Brother Luther that he was responsible for Bryson's death, that the whole monastery is responsible. Best not to show your faces right now."

"Where is Brother Luther?" Brother Ed couldn't believe this.

"He must have left about twenty minutes ago," Harry replied. "Look, it's nuts, but she's understandably out of it, and you . . . well, you all won't be helpful at this moment."

"Thank you." Brother Ed propelled Brother George into the old Volvo, another of the beat-up vehicles owned by the order.

Before he closed the door, Brother George said again, "Don't worry about this, Harry. Really."

It was a toss-up as to who felt most relieved when the two monks left, Brother George or Harry.

After another hour of organizing, cleaning, throwing garbage into the back of trucks so people could dispose of it, Harry and Fair drove back to the farm.

She'd told him about Tucker and Brother George.

"Not like Tucker. For some reason she's taken an extreme dislike to Brother George," he said.

"Won't anybody listen to me?" the dog whined in frustration.

Back at the farm, the dog relayed events to the two cats. All three animals agreed to continue being alert.

Finally in bed, Fair breathed a sigh of relief. "Emotional scenes exhaust me."

"Me, too. I don't know what's gotten into her. Well, she's drinking a lot. I expect she's been loaded ever since the news was broken to her. I don't know if she can control it anymore."

"I don't know, either, but Racquel, who's not a shrinking violet, still isn't the type to scream at somebody in front of everyone, no less."

Harry flopped back on two propped-up pillows. "What else can go wrong?"

She really should have known better than to ask that question.

30

Saturday, December 27, promised more snow. Cooper volunteered to work that weekend so she could have the next weekend off, when Lorenzo would be in town.

Harry told her of the scene at Racquel's. As it turned out to be a slow day, Cooper thought she'd drive to the monastery and ask a few more questions. Since no one was expecting her, she hoped to catch a few of the brothers off guard.

She knocked on the large wooden door.

No answer.

She knocked harder this time. Finally the door swung open.

Brother Luther invited her inside. "Is Brother Morris expecting you?"

"No."

"Let me see if he's available." Brother Luther started to shuffle off.

After a ten-minute wait in silence, Brother Morris swept in.

"Officer Cooper, please come into my office."

She followed him. "Where is everybody?"

"Working or praying. Here we are." He swept his arm outward, indicating where she should sit. "Can I get you anything?"

"No. I have a few questions. I won't take up much of your time."

"Anything to help. These events are beyond terrible." He settled in the oversize chair opposite hers.

"Are you aware of Racquel's outburst yesterday?"

"Brother Luther told me. The poor woman. I'd called on her that morning and she showed no hostility toward me."

"Dr. Deeds treated many of the brothers, did he not?"

"He was extremely generous."

"Did you ever have occasion to be with him during such times?"

This surprised Brother Morris. "No."

"Did you ever see him in the hospice?"

"Yes. He tended to our patients sometimes."

"Was any patient ever angry with him?"

"No. Quite the contrary."

"Did you ever hear any whispers of Dr. Deeds making a mistake? Say a mistake that cost a patient his or her life?"

This again surprised Brother Morris. "No. Again, Deputy Cooper, it was quite the reverse. He was above reproach in his profession."

"Ever hear or suspect he was having an affair or had had affairs?"

A silence followed this.

Brother Morris cleared his throat. "People talk."

"Tell me."

Shifting uneasily in his chair, he finally spoke. "There was talk about a liaison with a very pretty nurse. But you always hear that type of gossip. I certainly never suspected him of anything improper. I never even saw him flirting, and most everyone does that."

"No trouble with your brothers?"

"No. Granted, Dr. Deeds wasn't always sweetness and light. He was accustomed to giving orders." He smiled. "I half-expected him to yell out, 'Stat.' He was a caring physician. Bryson truly cared about his patients' welfare. I can't believe he would be murdered, but then I can't believe Brother Christopher and Brother Speed are gone, either."

"Do you know what an obol is?"

"Of course. In ancient Greece, it was placed under the deceased's tongue so they could pay Charon to ferry them across the

River Styx. Why?"

"Brothers Speed and Christopher and Dr. Deeds all had an obol under their tongues."

Brother Morris paled slightly. "How very strange."

"Racquel thinks all these murders point here."

He met her eyes. "They do. But why?"

"I hope to find out. Brother Morris, I don't think there is a human being alive who doesn't harbor some secrets. If you've been withholding something, please tell me. If it's something illegal, I'll do what I can for you. Given the situation, I need all the help you can give me."

He sighed deeply. "I would have told you by now if there was something. That doesn't mean a brother might not be covering up something, but there are no flashing red lights. The only thing that I return to is that Racquel was quite suspicious of Bryson. That's not a secret, but perhaps she saw demons when there were none."

"Perhaps, but there's certainly a demon out there now."

31

In the course of his practice, Bryson Deeds had treated people from all over the country. As they flew in to pay their respects, the house was never empty, which was a good thing, as it provided a distraction for Racquel. Miranda's idea about the food turned out to be a good one. After St. Luke's Sunday service, Harry and Fair swung by the Deedses' house to deliver the food they'd kept overnight.

Racquel appeared more in control. The Haristeens stayed briefly, making sure that Miranda didn't need anything.

Both breathed a sigh of relief when they walked through the door to their house.

"It'll be worse after the funeral." Fair untied his silk necktie. "People go home; your close friends call on you but, over time, they return to their normal routine. Then it really starts to sink in."

"Does." Harry pulled her slip over her

head. "I'll do the barn chores. I know you've got billings to send out."

"It can wait."

She pulled on her long, warm socks, followed by a quilted long-sleeve undershirt. "Racquel's been unhappy for months, maybe longer. I didn't see it then. I see it now."

"Socially she seemed fine."

"Most of us can pull it together socially. Looking back, though, I can see that she's been increasingly unhappy, reaching for the bottle too much, I guess. She complained about Bryson a lot. Now I expect she feels guilty about it and has no chance to make it up to him." She shrugged. "After this last week, I sure count my blessings."

"I do, too." He leaned over and kissed her. "You know, it's snowing again."

She looked out the window. "I'll be."

"Hey, let's do the chores, then I'll make a steak on the grill."

The grill was on the back lawn.

"Fair, it's colder than a witch's bosom."

He laughed. "Yeah, but the grill will work no matter what. You make a salad and then we can watch the movie I rented."

"You didn't tell me you rented a movie."

"Every now and then it's good to surprise you."

"What is it?"

"It's about the partnership of Gilbert and Sullivan. Since you love their work so much, especially *The Mikado,* I figured it'd be worth a look. Alicia saw it and said it was one of the best films she's ever seen about creativity."

"Sounds intriguing. What's the name?"

"Topsy-Turvy."

That phrase would apply to the unfolding drama right here in Crozet.

32

On Monday, December 29, people kept talking about the weather and the murder of Dr. Bryson Deeds. The weather remained the main topic, particularly since large apple groves, hay fields, timber, corn, and soybeans added to people's purses.

Rick and Cooper drove up the mountain, subpoena in hand. Thanks to Cooper's urgings, Rick had sent a young officer to watch over Harry so Fair could get back to work.

"Coop, you have a way of pushing me in the right direction."

"As long as I don't push you in front of a car." She smiled.

"When you called me after seeing Brother Morris, at first I didn't think too much about it. Then I remembered that charity for dying children, remember?"

"Yeah, back in 1994. The lady from Connecticut who set up the riding program for dying kids. Slick, slick, slick."

"She gets money for calm horses, a contractor builds a riding ring, another a barn, people see photos of these little kids hanging on to horses, and the money just pours in. All you have to do is show a picture of a child and people become instant suckers." He sighed. "So I thought, what are the Brothers of Love doing? Sitting, praying, holding the dying. Granted, a dying adult lacks some of the heart-tugging appeal of a six-year-old hurtling toward the red exit light, but still, families grateful for their service might give large sums, and I'm willing to bet a tank of gas —"

She interrupted. "That much?"

He grimaced. "That much. One tank of gas that a lot have enriched the monastery's coffers. Even the name 'Brothers of Love' could be a ploy."

"Didn't that woman, Kendra Something, walk off with close to three million smackers?" Cooper couldn't imagine having such a sum all to one's self.

"Damn straight she did. But she wasn't as smart as she thought she was. They picked her up in '97 in Belize. Sure lived the good life until then."

"You know, if I were going to be a crook, I'd go the charity route, too. It's the easiest way to steal. For one thing, accounting practices are different for 501(c)3 nonprofit corporations." She mentioned not-for-profit corporations that are charities. "For another thing, people want to help, so you appeal to their higher instincts and lighten their purses. Beats armed robbery."

"Except for robbing a bank or a Brinks truck. Gotta admit, there's glamour to that, as long as no one is killed. Takes brains, planning, guts, and cool, cool nerve. When I think of the thousands of perps I've talked to in my career, most of them evoke disgust or fury. But those guys, I grant them a backhanded admiration."

"Yeah, I can see that." She sat up straighter. "Well, we're here. Want me to wear my coat, keep my sidearm concealed, or do you want me to go in exposed?" She grinned at that.

"If you went in truly exposed, I expect half of those guys would run screaming for their rooms. The other half would run for you."

"What a pretty thing to say." Cooper evoked the old phrase used to great effect by Southern women for generations. One's tone indicated exactly how one felt about whatever had been said.

"Go in with sidearm showing. Just in case." He cut the motor and they both sprang out.

Cops surf adrenaline surges. While the willingness to face violence and personal danger is part of their personalities, it's also part of the high.

Rick knocked on the door. Knocked again.

At last the door opened and Brother Luther stood before them, dried blood on the side of his head, a shiner coming up, too.

"Brother Luther, what's happened?" Rick quickly stepped inside, as did Cooper.

"Brother Morris and three of the brothers have disappeared. Brother Sheldon, Brother Howard, and Brother Ed rounded up whoever is left."

"Why didn't you call me?"

"Because I was knocked out, and the others had been locked in their rooms. I finally found the keys."

"Where are the brothers?"

"In the kitchen." Brother Luther led them there without being asked.

Shocked faces turned toward the sheriff and his deputy.

Brother Sheldon wailed, "We're ruined!"

"Will you kindly shut up." Brother Ed's nerves were frayed enough; he couldn't withstand increased histrionics.

"Let him be, Brother Ed," Brother Howard, sagging in his bulk, said. "Sheriff, we were going to call you, but first we wanted to figure out what happened."

The other brothers nodded in agreement.

Cooper flipped open her notebook.

Rick began. "When did you discover you were locked in?"

"This morning. Rose for matins and couldn't open the door," Brother Howard, in charge due to his strong personality, informed them.

"They did it in the middle of the night," Brother Ed, furious, spat out.

"Brother Luther, how did you wind up with jewelry?" Rick asked.

"Beg pardon?" Brother Luther's head hurt.

"Sorry: jewelry, wounds," Rick replied.

"I couldn't sleep. So I got up around midnight and went to my office. I double-checked the books. They balanced, but I wanted to be sure. I've had a funny feeling about money lately, and I've learned to trust my instincts. There was a knock on the door. I answered. Brother Morris stood before me and that's all I remember."

"Did he take the books?" Rick appeared relaxed, but he was certain he was on the right track, eager to den his quarry.

"No. Left them as he found them."

"Brother Luther, do you think he'd been

pilfering funds?" Rick folded his hands together.

"It's worse than that." Brother Luther's voice shook.

On cue, Brother Sheldon wailed, tears streaming down his cheeks. "I didn't know. I swear I didn't know."

"Shut up!" Brother Ed seized Brother Sheldon's arm, holding it in his vise grip. "None of us knew. Why the hell do you think we were left here?"

"It appears he left you funds to continue your work and to live here," Cooper interjected.

"We can scrape by," Brother Luther replied dourly.

"I thought your order had received big contributions," Rick said.

"Yes, and that's when I became suspicious," Brother Luther said. "Those checks were given directly to Brother Morris or Brother George. I never saw them. Brother Morris always said he instantly put them into bonds. What a fool I was."

"You couldn't have known," Brother Ed consoled him.

"I do the books. I should have asked to see those bonds. I didn't."

"If you did, you might be dead." Brother Sheldon's voice lifted to the teary note.

Brother Ed cast him a stern eye. "You've got a point there, Brother Sheldon."

Calmly and deliberately, Rick asked, "Do you know where the money is?"

"Presumably with Brother Morris and Company." Brother Luther dropped his head in his hands. "I think it's a lot of money."

Rick glanced at Cooper, a hint of triumph in his face, which soon enough shifted to disbelief. "So people gave large sums in gratitude for your services in Brother Morris's name."

"No, Brother Morris isn't that dumb. He had to have an account with a bank or with a brokerage house similar to the one here." Brother Luther was sharp as a tack in his own way.

"What do you mean?" Rick unfolded his hands.

"Since I never saw the account, I can't give you a specific name, but an easy one would be to have the checks made out to BOL instead of Order of the Brothers of Love." Brother Luther's mind crept into underhanded accounting byways in an attempt to figure this out.

"A fairly straightforward scam." Rick's eyes met each brother's gaze.

"No. It's far more clever." Brother

Luther nodded to Brother Howard, who took over.

"My task for the order involved meeting people. You might say I am our public relations expert. I scheduled Brother Morris, I called on people. Brother George did, too, and I began to notice over the last two years . . . well, let me say that it wasn't obvious to me at first, since my mind doesn't run on that track."

Rick almost uttered the words, "What track?" but he waited patiently.

"I swear I didn't know," Brother Sheldon whimpered again.

"I called on the more middle-class people. Brother Morris and Brother George called on the richer ones."

"I'm not sure what the significance is," Rick replied honestly.

"Bigger checks, obviously, but I also think that Brother Morris and Brother George identified people with Achilles' heels." He paused. "I expect they threatened to expose them."

Cooper half-smiled. "Lucrative."

Rick continued questioning. "What kind of Achilles' heels?"

Brother Luther answered. "Gambling. Affairs. Shady business deals. And some of the affairs were married men with other men."

"How do you know that?" Rick pressed.

Brother Sheldon, misty-eyed again and looking guilty, confessed, "Brother Christopher told me."

"Brother Sheldon, you withheld evidence." Rick sounded stern.

"How could I have revealed that?"

"What did Brother Christopher have to do with it?"

"He owed money," Brother Sheldon said.

"To whom?"

"Alex Corbett." Brother Sheldon's chin wavered again.

"Don't start blubbering, Brother Sheldon." Brother Howard pointed a finger at him.

"Oh, shut up." Brother Sheldon surprised everyone, then turned to Rick. "Alex runs a little betting business: football, horses, any large sporting event. Brother Christopher couldn't resist the idea of winning money."

"So?" Rick shrugged.

"He didn't win." Brother Sheldon stated what he thought was obvious. "He had to pay it off somehow."

"How did he do that?" Rick kept his voice even.

"Sex for money." Brother Sheldon cast down his eyes. "It was wrong, but I wasn't going to rat on a friend."

"With women?" Rick had to admire Brother Sheldon's loyalty, even if somewhat misplaced.

"One man."

"Let me be clear: Christopher Hewitt sold his body to a man?"

"He didn't like it but the money was good. The man was head over heels." Brother Sheldon wanted to make sure no one thought Brother Christopher was gay. "Brother Christopher was weak where money was concerned."

"Who was his partner?"

"I'm not sure."

"Guess." Rick pushed harder.

"Bill Keelo or Bryson Deeds."

Rick's eyebrows shot up. "Your reasons?"

"Those were the men I saw him with, and they became increasingly helpful to our order."

Brother Howard butted in. "You think Brother Morris figured it out?"

"Of course," Brother Sheldon replied.

"Blackmail." Brother Luther shuddered. "I knew it!"

"Why didn't you come forward?" Rick forced his anger down.

"Didn't know for sure."

Cooper asked, "Was Brother Speed in debt, too?"

Brother Sheldon nodded. "He bet on the ponies." He sighed deeply. "Money. Money is the root of all evil."

"So they just wanted to pay off their debts?" Rick asked.

"Yes. They swore they'd stop gambling." Brother Sheldon had believed them.

"And Brother Speed . . . uh, serviced a man, too." Rick said more than asked, as he watched Cooper's pencil fly over her notebook.

"The money is with men, Sheriff. I don't think women will pay a lot for sex," Brother Howard interjected.

"So it seems." Rick was surprised, for he didn't see this coming. "Speed's client?"

"Either Bryson or Bill," Brother Sheldon answered.

"And Bill and Bryson knew about each other." Rick focused on Sheldon.

"They'd met the brothers together. At the Christmas tree farm or at the hospice. And they had good reasons to be there. They didn't arouse suspicion."

Brother Luther allowed himself an acid comment. "Bill Keelo tried to cover himself by being publicly homophobic. Ass."

Brother Sheldon, scandalized at the language, chided, "That's enough."

"Two men are dead and you're worried

that I said 'ass'?" Brother Luther snorted.

"So the question is, who was blackmailed and who killed?" Rick rubbed his jaw.

"Well, I can tell you Brother Christopher never blackmailed anyone." Brother Sheldon got misty again. "He tried to reform. He did. But easy money corrupted him. The flesh is weak."

"Obviously." Cooper's comment was fact.

"Blackmail." Brother Luther said the chilling word again and shook his head.

"I don't know if the order can recover from this," Brother Howard mournfully said.

Brother Luther replied, "People will always need help with the dying."

Driving down the mountain, Rick immediately sent out a call to pick up Brother Morris and his cohorts. Clever though the opera singer might be, hiding that bulk could prove very difficult.

"Think we'll get him?"

"Yeah, but I don't know when." Rick noticed how the water running over the rocks on the mountainside had turned to blue ice. "I hope we can get him to tell us exactly who they blackmailed. And mind you, Coop, this doesn't solve the murders."

Rick then called to have Bill Keelo and Alex Corbett picked up for questioning.

"They might be with Racquel," Cooper suggested.

"We'll swing by, then."

33

People continued to come and go at the Deedses', food being devoured with each successive wave of visitors. Racquel seemed more level, less prone to outbursts, at least so far. People understood that a sudden death unnerves those close to the deceased. Everyone made allowances for her.

Rick instructed the officers he called in to form a barrier on both ends of the street. He also sent some on foot to the back of the house, in case Bill or Alex made a run for it.

He parked the squad car alongside another car immediately in front of the house. Cooper couldn't get through on the Deedses' phone or Harry's cell, but she was right in thinking Bill and Alex were both there.

"Let's see if we can't do this calmly."

Coop, seeing Harry's truck as well as those of their friends, truly hoped this would be the case.

They knocked on the door, and Jean Keelo

opened it. Initially, she wasn't surprised to see them, assuming they'd come to pay their respects.

This changed when Rick whispered, "Do you think you can get your husband and Alex Corbett to the front door without arousing suspicion?"

Too late, for Biddy Doswell, not one to turn from any heightened emotion, squealed as she caught sight of Rick in the front hall. "Sheriff Shaw, how good of you to come."

Harry, in the kitchen with Mrs. Murphy, Pewter, and Tucker, heard Biddy bray.

"Bother." Harry sighed.

Cooper saw Bill in the dining room when she made her way through the people. She whispered to him, "Come with me."

"Why?" A belligerent note crept in his voice.

"It's better if you do. I'm sure you can give us the information we need. If you resist, I will arrest you. How will that look?"

Bill blanched. "I have a right to know what this is about."

"The murders."

"I have nothing to do with that." He was really belligerent now.

"Well, you were sleeping with Christopher Hewitt and maybe Brother Speed, too."

His face crumpled. He whispered, "I'll go."

"Do you know where Alex is?"

"With Racquel."

He followed Cooper to the foyer, where she opened the door. Bill was surprised to see an officer standing outside.

"Take him in." Cooper stepped back inside.

Racquel, ears perked up, cast her eyes upward as the two officers came into the room. She assumed, like everyone else, they were paying a social call.

Harry had left the kitchen, joining everyone in the living room. She observed Cooper's face and realized this was not a social call.

Cooper walked over to Alex, who was standing behind Racquel. As she whispered to him, his face registered fear.

"Something's up," Mrs. Murphy said, and her two friends felt it, too.

Rick leaned down. "Mrs. Deeds, could we have a moment of your time?"

"Now?" Her face registered suspicion while she tried to look a proper widow.

"We have some urgent questions. I'm very sorry, but it's critical we talk to you now in private." Rick's voice stayed low.

Racquel shot up, pushing him away. To his extreme embarrassment — for he had never considered the possibility — she snatched his revolver right out of the holster and grabbed Harry, who had come up to stand next to her.

Putting the gun to Harry's head with her right hand while wrapping her left arm around Harry's throat, she said in a not-unpleasant voice, "Harry, I truly like you, but you're my shield. Don't be stupid. I don't want to shoot you, but I will."

Harry, speechless because Racquel's left arm pressed hard against her throat, backed up as Racquel walked backward.

"Mrs. Deeds, don't make the situation worse than it is. Let her go," Rick commanded.

"No." Racquel kept backing up, looking over her shoulder. She shouted to her visitors, "Don't try anything. All I want is to get out of here and get away. Keep your distance and no one will get hurt." She looked at her two sons. "Boys, I can explain this later. Stay where you are. I don't want you in the middle of this."

They didn't even twitch.

"We could rush her," Pewter suggested.

"Need a better spot with less people." Mrs. Murphy assessed the situation.

"I can get behind her and trip her," Tucker offered. *"Then you two can rip her face off while I turn her legs into hamburger."*

"Our best chance is the back door, when she has to reach back for it. If she turns around, then Harry will be in front of her. That won't work for Racquel. She'll have to open the door while still facing the people," Mrs. Murphy said.

Without further coordination, the three animals silently hurried to the back door.

As Racquel continued to carefully back up, she said in a normal conversational voice to Harry, "I don't know how you accepted Fair as you did. In some ways I admire you for it. In other ways, I think you're a fool. Once a player, always a player. But let me tell you, so at least one person knows why I did what I did: Bryson was despicable. Completely despicable."

They reached the back door and, before getting her hand on the knob, Racquel slightly loosened her grip on Harry's throat.

Hoping to distract her, to slow her down, Harry rasped, "You killed them, didn't you?"

"Yes. Although I may have made a mistake with Christopher. Too late now." Her voice was almost cheerful. Her heel struck Tucker, who was lying down. The corgi stood up and bit her calf.

As Racquel started to tumble backward, Mrs. Murphy leapt up toward her face, delivering a slashing blow, while Pewter sank two serious fangs into the flesh between Racquel's thumb and forefinger.

Racquel still held the gun in her hand, which was pulled downward. She pressed the trigger without taking aim, shooting a hole in the floor.

Harry wrenched free. The cats now attacked Racquel's face, and Tucker, with greater jaws and more pressure per square inch, clamped onto her gun hand, biting so hard she severed a tendon and ripped through other muscles. Her grip shredded, Racquel dropped the gun. The mighty little corgi grabbed it in triumph and gave it to Harry. Harry quickly turned it on Racquel, who was still trying to swat away the cats.

"Mrs. Murphy, Pewter, let her go," Harry commanded.

"Oh, pooh," Pewter fussed, for her blood-lust was up.

Mrs. Murphy ripped out her claws. Pewter, knowing she had to as well, did, but not without the satisfaction of noticing some tiny bits of flesh dangling from them.

Rick and Cooper, who had followed from a distance so as not to provoke Racquel to harm Harry, now rushed forward.

Rick took back his gun.

Harry, wisely, said nothing.

Cooper had Racquel on her feet. The

woman's well-tended face was bleeding all over her and the floor, and her right hand shook with pain.

"Folks, after Sheriff Shaw puts Racquel in the squad car, best you all return home or to your hotels." Miranda, now out of the kitchen, took charge.

Coop called out to Harry, "Go home. I'll catch up with you later."

Harry knelt down to thank her animal friends, then stood up to follow Cooper's orders.

Jean seconded Alicia's request. "People, none of us knows what's going on. Please go. I'll call you if I know anything." She turned to Alicia. "I'll stay with the boys until their grandparents get here. They said they'd be coming by at about five."

Once out the door, Pewter puffed up. *"She didn't have a chance."*

"Yes, Rocky." Mrs. Murphy smiled.

34

Hurrying home after his wife called and thankful that no equine emergencies had sprung up, Fair blew through the door. "Honey! Honey, where are you?"

"In the living room."

He walked in to find Harry stretched out on the couch, two cats on her chest and one corgi on her feet. "Don't get up. Tell me everything."

"I will. Could you bring me something to drink? I'm a little shaky. I don't have a scratch on me except for my head, but that doesn't count."

"I'll bring you some hot tea with lemon and a tiny touch of something special."

Harry rarely drank, but Fair thought a dollop of good whiskey wouldn't be amiss. As he heated the water, Coop drove up.

Once in the house, Cooper closed the door and leaned against it.

"Harry, bless you."

"Drink?" Fair was anxious to know what had happened.

"Beer. I want a big, fat, cold beer."

He opened the refrigerator and handed her a St. Pauli Girl, her favorite.

Within minutes all were seated in the living room, Harry upright now, her feet on the coffee table.

Cooper first told them about visiting the monastery and the forlorn abandoned brothers who'd been locked into their rooms, except for Brother Luther, who'd been knocked out. "As it happens, the North Carolina state police picked up the perps as they headed for the coast. Brother Morris wanted the others to disperse, but no one trusted him to give them the money once they were safe. A falling-out among thieves." She half-smiled, then took a sip. "And Brother Luther and Brother Howard were right: Brother Morris had a separate account; he was definitely blackmailing men. But he's not a killer."

"Good Lord," Fair exclaimed.

"Where does Racquel come in?" Harry burst with curiosity.

"Bryson had had affairs at the hospital. The ones she initially pounced on over the years were with women. But as time went on, he couldn't submerge his true nature.

She sensed it. Over the last year and a half, his constant visits to the monastery for 'medical reasons' sent her red flags up. She started snooping. He really did think he was smarter than anyone else, didn't take too many precautions. He assumed no one would dream he had fallen in love with Speed. Racquel found condoms, the occasional cryptic note in what seemed to be a man's handwriting. Bryson made two fatal mistakes: he underestimated his wife, and he fell in love with Speed. At least that's what Racquel says.

"Racquel initially thought he was in love with Christopher." Cooper took a breath. "She was so humiliated that her husband was sleeping with a man that she lost it. She confronted him. He denied it."

"Did she overpower them in some fashion?" Fair asked.

"No. Racquel is very attractive. She offered herself to them. Remember, both men like women, or liked them. All she had to do was slip behind them and slit their throats before they knew what hit them. Neither man dreamed he was in danger."

"Didn't their murders upset Bryson? If he was in love with Speed he would be devastated," Fair said.

"He tried to hide it, but he was. His suppressed grief made her even angrier," Cooper said.

"And Bryson didn't suspect his wife?" Harry wondered how Bryson could be so obtuse.

"He was getting nervous, but he didn't think Racquel was the killer. He thought he had her under his thumb. Apart from his inborn arrogance, he had a touch of smugness about women. He thought men were superior, or so Racquel says. He didn't treat her badly, but she felt tremendous humiliation, and her desire for revenge overcame even her maternal affection for the boys. She never thought she'd be caught, though. She was so blinded by rage she didn't think about being separated from her sons."

"Those poor kids. Their mother killed their father. They love both parents." Harry felt terrible for the boys. "Do you think Racquel would have killed me?" she asked Cooper.

"Probably. I don't think she wanted to, but if it came down to your life versus her freedom, she would have shot you."

"Lucky I have fast friends." Harry dangled her arms over each kitty, now in her lap, and Tucker on the floor.

"No one messes with us," Pewter bragged.

"Here's something: Brother Morris won't confess to blackmail. Big surprise. He only says people gave as their hearts moved them."

"That's not what was moving," Fair said laconically.

The two women laughed.

Harry then inquired, "He's not saying where the money is, is he?"

"Hell, no. He'll hire a great lawyer, serve his time, and come out to unearth the money. Here's something else: he admitted that Bryson was generous and that Bill Keelo made a sizable Christmas donation."

"Bill is currently in jail, since he was uncooperative." Cooper liked the idea of the lawyer cooling his heels. "Alex swears he's not involved, but he fits the description of the man who accompanied Racquel to the coin store." She paused. "He's in love with her, of course."

"Bill Keelo." Harry was surprised.

"Hoping to draw attention from himself, all that homophobic rant." Cooper smiled ruefully. "People can be pretty nasty. When they can't face who and what they are, it's a real cluster you-know-what."

"Yep." Harry liked the tang in her tea.

"I'm willing to bet that Racquel's lawyer will use in her defense that she was frightened that Bryson would commit incest with their sons." Cooper knew how legal things worked.

"Gross." Harry wrinkled her nose.

"And it will be very effective." Fair, too, had seen enough legal arguments to know some slick lawyer could get Sherman's March to the Sea reduced to trespassing.

"So Bryson never went out for milk?"

"He did. But he thought he was going for an assignation at Barracks Road. Racquel had sent him a text message, name withheld, to meet for sex. The man was a fool for sex. She howled with laughter when she described walking up to the Tahoe. She'd parked behind the buildings, then walked out into the parking lot. She said if she sits in jail forever, she'll cherish that moment when he realized the game was up and he wasn't half as smart as he thought he was. She had a gun on him and marched him to the fountain. Then she put the gun to his temple, told him to hold still, and slit his throat. He didn't expect that, either. She's totally unrepentant."

"And the boys will never admit their mother left the house on Christmas Eve. I expect they knew she'd left the house," Harry said.

"Probably. What a burden they'll carry."

"What's the significance of the obol?" Fair inquired.

"To throw us off. She won't tell us who accompanied her when she stole them. She laughed again when we brought that up. She said they'll all go to hell and she paid the fare. She's gleeful."

Suddenly Pewter shot off Harry's lap, raced for the tree, and climbed to the top, where she batted the gold star. *"I'm the top of the top."*

"Demented." Tucker sighed.

"I saved the day! Me. Me. Me."

"There's no living with her." Tucker sighed.

"Can't beat 'em, join 'em." Mrs. Murphy leapt off the sofa and climbed the tree, hanging on the trunk across from Pewter.

The Christmas tree swung to and fro, the balls tinkling when they touched one another.

Harry got up and reached into the tree to steady it by grasping the trunk. Her reward was to be pricked by the sharp needles.

The cats hollered, *"We're the tops, we're the cat's pajamas."*

It was just as well that Cole Porter had gone to his reward and that Harry had no idea what those two were shouting about.

Ho Ho Ho

Isn't Christmas the best? A trimmed tree to climb, presents to shred, food that falls under the table or is helpfully pushed off. Christmas is a cat's favorite holiday.

There is one little quibble I have with how humans view Christmas. Who do you think kept mice away from Baby Jesus? Who curled up in His cradle to keep Him warm? The swaddling clothes weren't worth squat. A cat. Oh sure, there was a donkey there and a cow and chickens, but it was a cat that did the work. A few humans remember because a tiger cat with an M on its forehead is a descendant of Mary's cat.

Even if you don't have a Mary's cat, do shower your puss with tuna, chicken, beef, ham, capons, goose, catnip, and warm fuzzies to sleep on. It's the Christian thing to do.

Sneaky Pie

Dear Reader,

For once I've read Sneaky's missive to you all and I agree one hundred percent. Let me add one thing: give to your local humane shelter. Give as generously as you can. Some of the cats and dogs are there because their owner has passed away or is ill and can no longer attend to them. Most are there because of crass human irresponsibility. Personally, I'd like to bring back the stocks and put these sorry so-and-so's in them for all to see. It's humans who maim and abandon pets, not the reverse. So do remember Mary's cat and all the others who are temporarily dependent on you. As Blanche DuBois said, "I have always depended on the kindness of strangers."

Merry Christmas.
Happy New Year.

ABOUT THE AUTHORS

Rita Mae Brown is the bestselling author of several books. An Emmy-nominated screenwriter and poet, she lives in Afton, Virginia. Her website is www.ritamaebrown.com. She does not own a computer. God willing, she never will. Sometimes the website manager sends your queries. The safest way to reach her is in care of Bantam Books.

Sneaky Pie Brown, a tiger cat born somewhere in Albemarle County, Virginia, was discovered by Rita Mae Brown at her local SPCA. They have collaborated on seventeen Mrs. Murphy mysteries: *Wish You Were Here; Rest in Pieces; Murder at Monticello; Pay Dirt; Murder, She Meowed; Murder on the Prowl; Cat on the Scent; Pawing Through the Past; Claws and Effect; Catch as Cat Can; The Tail of the Tip-Off; Whisker of Evil; Cat's Eyewitness; Sour Puss; Puss 'n Cahoots; The Purrfect Murder;* and *Santa Clawed,* in addition to *Sneaky Pie's Cookbook for Mystery Lovers.*